Tips on how to lose your spouse

By Mathew Walker

Copyright © 2024 Mathew Walker

Cover designed by Nathan Gordon, SITEBEAST - hello@sitebeast.co.uk

All rights reserved. No portion of this book may be reproduced, or stored in a retrieval system, or transmitted in any form or by any means, electronic, mechanical, photocopying, recording, or otherwise without written permission from the author.

This is a work of fiction. Names, characters, places, and incidents are either the product of the author's imagination or are used fictitiously. Any resemblance to actual persons, living or dead, events, or locales is entirely coincidental.

1st Edition *published 2024*

For my wife (who told me to "just write that book")

To my sons (who slowed down the writing process somewhat)

I love you.

Extra special thanks to:

Sam North (your eye for detail and dedication to my project was invaluable)

Nate Gordan (Once again, as many times before, you have leant me you creative genius, the cover is sick!)

Now just read the bloody story!

Enjoy

HIS STORY

Chapter One

Well, isn't this is awkward.

I really wish I could just hang my head in shame but there is a little pool of sick by my feet being slowly soaked up by my trainers and subsequently seeping into my socks, serving as a constant reminder of the…, let's call it 'incident'. I can only blame myself; I spoke this into existence, 'do we have to get the boat? I get seasick!' Maybe if I hadn't moaned so much and not thought about it constantly it wouldn't have come to fruition, but in actuality, it was a complete self-fulfilling prophecy. But then again, not moaning, and self-sabotaging would be breaking a habit of a lifetime. I feel every single bump and current of the ocean like walking across a cobbled street in plimsols, why am I so hypersensitive to this? Everyone else was enjoying the journey, until I swiftly put a stop to that.

Thankfully my daughter is sat in her baby travel seat to the side of the boat securely strapped in, and my wife is sat at the front of the boat about 8 rows away from me. She knows I get seasick, and as I have said, I had moaned about it non-stop in the lead up to the holiday, so she opted to sit at the other side of the boat and pretend to not know me. That's fine though. At least this shame is mine and not something that will tarnish the entire family.

My rationale for sitting at the back of the boat was that if I sat near the exit, I would be fine because there would be a quick way out. What I did not know was this particular door was just the exit for when the journey was over and cannot be opened while the ship is at sail, the exit for the decking was located to the top left of the seating area, had I known that I would have sat there and then there would have been no problem, I would feel it coming, bolt out the door as quick as an Olympic sprinter and feed the fish with my regurgitation.

What transpired was this, I figured that with 10 minutes of the journey remaining, despite feeling very sick since setting sail, I could hold it all in, and I was very wrong about that, especially as the boat hurdled a few 'keen' waves. I vomited on my feet but instantly knew more was coming, so I then ran to what I thought was the exit to the decking while a member of staff violently waved their hands and repeatedly shouted "No!" Too late, I was sick there. Someone, I don't know who, shouted, "the side of the boat", I darted to the right, nope, sick again, a teenager in an oversized hoodie and headphones on then shouted very loud, "the other side dickhead". Nothing beats being called names by someone at least 15 years your junior while being violently sick.

I got to the other side of the boat, but too late to locate the door and was sick a good three more times. The cabin looked like it had been victim to some form of spewing Catherine Wheel, and I now have the indignity of being sat by the exit while making sheepish eye contact with my fellow passengers as they exited the boat having been sat in my stench for at least 9 minutes.

A great start to the family holiday.

The first thing I do on dry land is take off my wife's old pregnancy anti-sickness bands and throw them in the bin, calling them useless in the process. As they had failed me, I felt at least having the last word would help me scrape back some dignity while offloading my frustration, not that it lasted long because I instantly felt immature. Following them into the bin were my soggy socks and smelly footwear. Luckily our accommodation is only a short walk from the harbour. My wife was already striding off up ahead on her phone, probably calling her mum to let her know what a disaster the journey had been, but ultimately relaying the message that we had arrived safely.

As I slowly moved forward barefoot with the baby in the pram and luggage in tow my wife turned and looked at me, gave me a sympathetic look, and continued talking on the phone. I overheard her say something about finding a place to eat for this evening. Having been married for 3 years and together for 6 I knew that this meant she will go and explore and book us a table for tonight while me and the baby check into the B&B. It is a level of telepathy that only comes with a long-term relationship, unspoken tasks, and actions.

I can recall the first time I saw my wife, that image of her has become a happy place for me and it was essentially one of those moments which seemed perfect whenever I reminisce. We met by chance in a coffee shop, I was extremely hungover and was recharging before facing a stroll home. I didn't even have a job at the time, and my mental health was very poor. My wife, at the time was just an incredibly attractive stranger waiting in line for a brew, she had a handbag over her left arm, laptop tucked under her right arm and mobile phone crushed between her shoulder and ear. It was love at first sight...for me anyway. For her it was most likely a mixture of who is this mess, and what is that smell.

Chapter Two

Arriving at the B&B I was immediately satiated with this stunning, Tudor cottage located by the harbour. Some serious craftsmanship had gone into maintaining this building that looked old, but well loved. Me turning up smelling like sick and with no shoes on like I had been on a stag do really did not show this magnificent time capsule the respect it so richly deserved. It was a setting steeped in history and character, to an extent it almost looked unsafe as the beams across the doorway had begun to warp from years of weathering and the straw roof looked like it had been hacked at by a visually impaired lumberjack, but I loved it. It was hard to tell because I was still a little dizzy from the seasickness, but I am sure the building was leaning slightly. These are the types of places I want my daughter to see, not these bloody new builds with their perfect straight edges and plain décor, no, give us buildings with personality.

We entered the B&B ready to be bestowed by magic, well I was, the baby does not care, it did not disappoint inside. There was a patterned red rug stretching from the entrance to the reception area, it was faded around the edges and had bare patches through the centre where it had clearly been walked on many times. It had flowers and swirls repeated throughout and tiny symbols I did not recognise, but very nice detail indeed. The walls were encased in wooden panelling with dimly lit lights protruding from them. The reception area, which looked like a repurposed cloakroom, had lights on the wall which were designed to resemble candles and gave off a dim yet warm glow and an occasional flicker that cast a momentary shadow across the wall of an old-fashioned broom and oil lantern. I almost forgot it was glorious sunshine, sea, and boats outside, and felt like getting comfortable with a blanket and a good book. The walls were made of oak panelling and painted black and white to fit in with the Tudor theme and with each step, even barefoot, there was a slight creak. I felt like I had gone back in time, and I love it.

Approaching the desk, I noticed there were wet footprints on the carpet behind the till area, and there was an odd aroma, quite rustic but with elements of fish and iron. I was looking at the ensemble in the till area. There was an old-school bell which was placed below a solid brass antique rotary dial telephone, a parchment logbook with ink and quill, which confirmed to me that this place was committed to their old-fashioned theme, which is fantastic.

I tapped the bell and awaited a staff member to come and sign us in. There was a wait and then a faint creaking noise from around the back which developed into slow thudded footsteps. As if out of nowhere an old looking fisherman came to the reception. He did not smell good and instantly I knew this was whom the faint fish aroma was secreting from. I looked him up and down drinking in every detail, this was brilliant. He seemed to be dripping wet, although it was a lovely warm and dry day outside. Looking at his leather wellingtons boots, I knew exactly why the carpet had wet footprints Imprinted on it, although these had faded remarkably fast. I can't believe my wife was missing all this. What a show.

His clothes are very old fashioned which was fitting with the overall theme of the B&B, his thick cuffed turtleneck was complemented by a grey sweater and waterproof overalls. I admired his fisherman's hat which looked like it was from the 1920s, even the most daring men out there would not be able to style that out with such ease. He had gone to the extreme of making his outfit damp unless he genuinely was both a fisherman and B&B reception staff, it is a small island maybe the people here on Melas have to double up on jobs, maybe he owns the place? He moved slowly with his eyes fixed on me the entire time, he approached the counter, his mouth twitching like he wanted to welcome us, but I am assuming his tough fisherman image would not afford pleasantries. I thought I would get the ball rolling, "afternoon, love the apparel, and the decoration throughout is splendid. Anyway, I have a double room with a cot booked please".

At this stage I noticed he was carrying a small knife and was gripping it tightly, this disenchanted me as it did not seem very welcoming, I assume it had been used for, or, judging by the smell, is being used for gutting fish. This is guess work as I possess zero knowledge of fishing or sea fishing. Considering his wax coated anorak, and rugged white beard that was a tremendous testament to what I would envision a Victorian fisherman to look like, the knife tightly gripped in his hand did give off a serial killer vibe.

Perhaps I have watched too many documentaries with my wife.

Without speaking he turned and slid open a cabinet and grabbed a silver key attached to a black and white lighthouse keyring with a red number 9 on it. Another nice touch. He walked away from the till area and began staring down the corridor, I can only assume now that I was meant to follow him. As he trudged by me, I noticed a monochrome photograph on the wall of a group of old fishermen side by side holding up a pint of ale, he looked a lot happier in this photo than he does currently. But then again, don't we all with a pint of ale in our hand?

I picked up our luggage, which did look out of place in this historic setting with its neon pink Perspex coating, and accidentally dropped it down on my foot with a thud, "FUCK" I shouted, this journey has been a bloody nightmare so far. To add to the stressful situation mounting, the thud of my carelessness's combined with my loud profanity woke my daughter, and she began wailing like a laughing dolphin. At this, the old fisherman stopped in his tracks and turned to stare at my baby, he didn't speak or even smile, he just starred at her, his mouth began to twitch again, and he started to bare his teeth, his hand which was holding the knife began to shake, what was his problem?

I quickly stumbled over to the pram throwing myself within range to be impaled should this lunatic lunge at my baby. The fisherman moved back as if awoken from a trance. "Is there some kind of problem here? She's a baby, she cries", he was simply unfazed by my aggressive demeanour. He just began walking again, expecting me to follow. I watched him for a few seconds, confused and shaking a little from adrenaline, I don't care for confrontation, and then I took my daughter out of her pram and carried her, partly to calm me down but mainly it seemed the safest place to have her. It is difficult to settle in a B&B when the concierge could be a moot lunatic, but I was incredibly tired from all the travelling, along with the expected tiredness of having a young child. Perhaps I read too much into the situation, although he definitely did bare his teeth, maybe he hates babies?

Being a positive person, I noted to myself that at least I didn't have to unpack everything right now just in case my wife thinks we should find a different accommodation where a Victorian looking knife wilding manic doesn't act in such a way that you feel your child could be gutted like a…well you know, that one's too easy. I would expect such a place would not be hard to find.

I continue my painful trait of over thinking and analysis and I am now wondering if I may have panicked and overreacted, being such an anxious person, I often see dangers that may not actually be there. Maybe he just had a bit of a temper but surely, he wasn't going to impale my baby. Surely not. I was being ridiculous. We should stay here; it is a beautiful building.

I did unpack some socks and trainers; it is funny how being without something you would consider to be a basic standard of living becomes an absolute luxury when you have found yourself without it. I quickly rinsed my legs in the marble standalone bath, further falling in love with the aesthetics of this place. I dried myself from my shins to my toes and put on some fresh footwear which was accompanied by a fresh wave of optimism. Onwards and upwards, I was free from dry sick on my hairy legs, I was feeling a little better, and I had fresh socks and trainers on. Ready to get into holiday mode and have some fun.

Standing in front of the harbour being hypnotised by how the slight current manipulated the sun's reflection into an electric dance I felt that we had finally arrived, a calm had come over me, one hand was on the pram the other was holding an Ice Cream which came from a van with the charming name 'Mongers Cream' although it explains why you could buy a cone with flake or a tub of muscles.

This could still turn out to be a fantastic holiday, although I did have to pretend not hear someone saying, "that's that weirdo that was sick on the boat". I offered the baby a lick of ice cream, some people close by who presumably didn't have children gave me a dirty look as if my daughter had a pure Ice Cream diet, I couldn't resist playing up to this and promised my little one a milkshake with a slice of cake before bed. The nosey couple just shook their heads and walked off. I sniggered to myself and then looked down to my daughter. "Right then pumpkin, let's go and find Mummy

Chapter Three

"How many more steps?! Seriously, what the hell is this? Didn't realise we had to go to the beach via the Great Wall of China", and there I go, moaning again.

My wife turned to me with an expression on her face which indicates she is already sick of my grousing, regardless of how whimsical and sarcastic it may be. She makes, what is probably the correct decision, and ignores me. I noted how her dyed blonde hair effortlessly complemented the clear blue sky and gleaming sunshine, she perfectly coexisted with nature to light up the world. The slight breeze gave her hair a shining, electric, current as if she was in a shampoo advert. Thus, concluding my obsessive, inner monologue.

I continued complaining on the off chance that she would engage with, or at the very least empathise with me "how many more steps do I have to climb with this pram? I feel like we've been walking for miles to this beach already". Hindsight is throbbing in my temples and telling me I should have left the pram at the B&B and let the angry fisherman carve it up, that way I would not be dragging a set of tiny stubborn wheels up all these steps, and he might have some relief or form of anger management. I wonder if he is still thinking about me as much as I am thinking about him. I strangely feel a bit needy.

The wife seemed to be low on sympathy or still mad about 'sick gate' back on the boat because she just turned back and looked at me but said nothing, in fact I think I detected a slight dirty look. She carried on towards the beach with determination. Her face is flawless, she is so beautiful, even after all this time together she still makes my heart do a short, weird drumroll rhythm beat when I look at her. Coming to think of it, my left arm really hurts, oh shit, am I having a heart attack? They say if you love something too much it's guaranteed to kill you, and she definitely satisfies that criterion.

I assume she knows I am having some sort of inner soliloquy or maybe a panic attack and decided to continue walking. She knows it is best to just leave me to it at times like this. I guess I had better proceed with the pram and just focus on my breathing and the sounds of the ocean. Calm down. If I am having a heart attack, then I am going to die a hero and get this baby to the beach first. Although that would probably piss her off also, the determination of getting to the destination and then dropping dead, maybe I am an idiot.

I pushed hard on the pram as we had now entered an extra tenacious level of difficulty, the new challenge is forcing the wheels through thick yet soft sand. I gave the pram a big shove, but the wheels remained static, and I ended up with the pram handle embedded in my gut. As I knelt down hugging my ribs and wheezing from being winded, I was at least rewarded for my efforts by my baby laughing at me and kicking me playfully in the face. My wife clearly had no intention of breaking her stride to ask if I was okay, although she was quite far in front to be fair to her, she probably hasn't realised I have injured myself on the pram.

At this stage my logical thinking kicked in and dictated that I should turn the pram around and pull it rather than push. With sweat streaming down my forehead like a ceiling about to collapse from an upper floor flood I persisted with our endeavour. The sweat was stinging my eyes, I always thought the purpose of eyebrows was to capture sweat from your forehead. Is there something wrong with my eyebrows? Why is my face malfunctioning? Calm down.

Deep breaths, listen to the sea. Focus on the task at hand…read up online about eyebrows later though.

A quick glance over my shoulder confirmed my wife was significantly ahead of us, I couldn't even see her actually, but that is good news, it means the beach must be close by. But not before another set of bloody steps! I did not realise we were in Huairou; this is ridiculous. I say to my daughter, "when you are bigger you definitely owe me a few lifts, I don't care if it's by car, carriage or you just throw me over your shoulder as an old decrepit man and carry me, whatever, you owe me". I could have sworn she just rolled her eyes at me, very reminiscent of her mother. I continue navigating the pram on the steps.

Having completed the second set of steps I was greeted by yet another sandy pathway, my back groaned at the thought of dragging the pram further and I was sure my coccyx was protruding unusually. I looked down at my wife's footprints in the sand, such delicate imprints leaving a poetic impression until a strong wind or rain comes and removes all traces of us ever being here. I can't imagine my erratic tramlines of pram wheels is quite as picturesque as my wife's footprints, nor can I conceive the smell I am leaving behind is very pleasant either.

Such is the danger on having time to reflect, this confirmed that I am without doubt a needy person because I can't see my wife and it is making me feel very anxious. Although I do appreciate she is leading the way, and will have no doubt found us a brilliant spot on the beach. I do wish we had some form of agreement in place, much like a parent and toddler does, "you go ahead and lead the way my love,

BUT DON'T GO OUT OF SIGHT" does that make me a control freak? Or is this simply a biproduct of anxiety? Maybe I just need to fully focus on getting our daughter to the beach and stop having an ongoing conversation in my head, who knows maybe my wife would still be in sight if I managed myself better. I reassured myself that this constant self-reflection and over the top analysis was due to high levels of intelligence. I proceeded with the pram, embarrassed by my own ego.

My child and I finally reached the top of a sand dune which had a relatively kind decline towards the beach. I stood there, the king of the castle, breathing in the sea air, taking in the beautiful coastline with its gentle smooth sand interrupted by rock pools and those huge rock things that probably go very deep under the sand, like some form of stone-based iceberg. I stood taking in a panoramic view, I took slow steps, sure there is a crisp packet dancing to the invisible puppet strings of the ocean breeze, and there is one or two pop bottles left behind by some arsehole, but still, you can't beat nature! Oh, for fucks sake, is that a used condom?! I hate humans.

Right, there is clearly a joke about the beach and seamen here, but there is no time for that, I had better go find the wife.

Chapter Four

I don't think it is well enough documented just how difficult and awkward it is trying to locate someone on a beach. A busy beach anyway. I know my wife is here somewhere, but I can't look too much to the left because there is a group of women sunbathing. I can't look too much to the right because there's a group of teenagers, a few of whom look particularly menacing, and straight ahead of me are some young kids playing in a rockpool, which would be fine, but they are naked. So, if I look too hard in any general direction, I'll either be called a pervert, or potentially get beaten up, or worse of all be called a nonce.

I am sure if my eyes did stray too much to the left for too long my wife would suddenly appear, arms crossed, eyebrows raised awaiting an explanation. Alas, that is not a tactic I wish to employ. Just thinking about it makes me feel a bit nervous.

I abandoned the pram with a sense of great relief, I left it close enough to a random family so that it could feasibly belong to them, but not so close that it encroached on their personal space or violates social norms. As I continued my inner monologue chronicling the awkward beach search, daughter in arms, I realised I had walked too far in one direction when my wife could have easily gone the other way. I mean, there's a 50-50 chance and I over committed.

Being British I live by the code that; to get back to where I want to be I must walk in a large but gradual semi-circle and hope no one notices that I'm turning around. Spinning on the spot would out me as someone who is clearly lost, much to the amusement of strangers, and I will feel all their eyes burning into my back as I continued my walk. I did not need that kind of judgement and scrutiny right now, not today.

I began my subliminal 180 degree reroute, scanning the beach and keeping my eyes peeled, now, to my left there were men playing beach volleyball in their speedos, I am hoping my wife didn't notice this. To the right is an ice cream van which is both genius and puzzling. I can't fault the decision making of the ice cream lady for setting up there, the line of people speaks volumes of her business acumen, but I can't see any vehicle access to the beach, or any indication in the sand that a van had travelled across it?! However, that is not my concern so I will park it for now, no pun intended.

This is getting tedious; I am about 3 minutes away from engaging lunatic mode and just yelling her name aimlessly while squinting around the beach like an octogenarian using voice recognition on a TV remote. Ah, screw it, I'm going to go for it "Lainya? LAINYA??". Okay, good. I now have the attention of every single person on the beach, I will let my overactive anxiety take over from here then. My amygdala is screaming at me to just run into the ocean and drown myself to escape this predicament. Good job I have the little one in my arms.

Another 10 minutes pass and the predicament has now successfully transferred across from tedious to bullshit! This is straight up, bullshit! Where on earth is she?!

It feels like everyone is looking at me still which is embarrassing and for some reason makes me extra aware of every step I take, however, it does also confirm I shouted my wife loud enough that it should have got her attention. But nothing. And this is where panic really begins to settle in. My brain switches from mild separation anxiety to lost child, she can't be left or right of the beach unless she got here and sprinted across the sand like a Cheetah across the Sahara. And straight ahead is the ocean, so unless she'd sprinted ahead and dived into sea and swam half a mile, I can't fathom she did that, as spectacular as that may have been.

I briefly think of asking the lifeguard for some help, but I do not like the way the sun is bouncing off his pecks, I would feel like an ant hill under a magnifying glass, plus my adrenaline is flowing to an extent that if I spoke now my voice would come out with a squeaky quiver suggesting I am both prepubescent and scared, when I am only slightly one of these things. The last thing I need at this moment is to encourage his male bravado while I'm shaking with nervous adrenaline and holding my little girl. Concluding my private yet completely unnecessary character assassination of the lifeguard who is probably nice and professional I figure I should double back to look for my better half, maybe she went back the way we came to look for us?

I grab the pram and instantly feel the burn in the muscles that I had strained on the way to the beach, but my shoulders feel a bit lighter now I'm not holding the baby. I stand around aimlessly hoping she will appear, after a few minutes I decide enough time had passed for me to once again draw attention to myself, "LAINYA? LAINYA??" still no Lainya, although it did startle a young couple snogging each other's faces, so my top form of ruining happy holiday memories continues.

Some blokes would no doubt love to lose their wives, and I am certain nearly all women would rather lose their husbands than win the lottery. It will be no different for same sex couples either. But not me, no way, I am co-dependent and proud.

I challenge the upheaval of the sand dunes, the way we entered the beach, consistently losing my footing and sliding back slightly but taking big enough steps to be slowly moving in the right direction. If in doubt and completely clueless, retrace your steps. Fine detective work. I look left and right, and then suddenly something catches my eye. There is something knotted within in the marram grass. Something that really draws my attention, wait is that…I rush over, oh god, they are Lainya's flip flops.

Fuck!

Chapter Five

I can recall the exact moment my wife and I met. In terms of my fondest memories or greatest highlights of my life it is up there along with our wedding day and the birth of our little pumpkin. It was a life defining moment and changed my trajectory for the better and forever. She wouldn't like this, but I liken it to when you first see your football team play, the vibe in the stadium, your favourite player scoring a goal, that is a different kind of love, but it is a love. Her taste in sport is more boisterous than mine, she likes Rugby and UFC, I like Football and Tennis.

Like the genesis of all great romances, I was on a stag do in Sheffield city centre. Before you start trying to guess I'll tell you, she wasn't a barmaid, she wasn't a stripper, she wasn't on a hen do the same night and we crossed paths broke off from our respective groups and did our own thing, I didn't even meet her while on the stag do, the stag do is a small element, but it preceded the circumstance that fate crafted for me. For us.

The stag do itself was insane, it started like a regular night out, me and 'the lads' had a few drinks, we relentlessly took the piss out of the stag while repressing the thought that he was maybe further on in his life than us to the back of our minds. Then shots happened and the subsequent hours were a blur, I hit a wall…and then was sick against it. After throwing up I felt better and ready to continue drinking, the dizziness had faded away. Naturally I felt a little shame at what had happened, but I comforted myself with the thought that this was regular practice when I was 18 years of age so by backwords logic, I had not lost any form.

The night ended in the casino. A terrible, awful, moronic idea. I had never gambled before, I mean, I had taken a risk now and again, but I hadn't put money on sports events or set foot in a casino ever. I have an addictive personality and these places scared me. Such is the nature of being on a stag in which being 'one of the lads' has a direct correlation to surviving the evening I withdrew £200 from my remaining £250 overdraft and fell into the false arrogant bravado of believing I could turn this £200 into £10,000. That ambition died a death agonisingly quick; I then watched my mates make similar errors while thinking to myself that coin pusher machines in arcades are criminally unappreciated.

We had a couple of free drinks which I assume the casino would hope prompted us to make further drunken cash withdrawals and subsequent bets we couldn't afford and then before you know it those complementary free cocktails cost £60 each. But we were not daft, we don't know much but what we do know is when it's kebab time. In that respect, catastrophe was avoided.

Now, the walk from the casino to the kebab shop was a good laugh, a lot happened, but nothing 'noteworthy' happened just a lot of random football chants, more throwing up, and one of the lads got punched in the bollocks. It was pretty standard from there, kebab, taxis, stroll, sway, and stumble home, but for some reason, which I cannot quite remember I awoke the next morning on a park bench.

For this to have happened I must have been ludicrously intoxicated, not just the decision making, but the fact I cannot recall how or why I was there. But I did learn park benches are a secret life hack because I slept well. Really well actually. My suit had somehow remained crease free, my wallet was missing but I had £5 in pocket, my phone is also in my pocket but only has 10% battery life and my house key is in my sock. So, on the whole I would say it was not ideal but could have been worse.

I assumed I must have gotten out the taxi to be sick, or maybe I had already misplaced my wallet and realised I couldn't pay, and then being too tired to walk I would have seeked refuge on the bench, lucky for me those summer nights rarely drop below 16 degrees, so I was relatively comfortable. I took a quick selfie so I could examine my reflection, I can rule out being mugged as there isn't a bruise or scratch on me, the missing wallet will be down to me being careless. I was familiar with my surroundings. Home was a good 4 miles from here, so logic dictated I went to the coffee shop first before I begin the crusade to my residence. And that is where I met Lainya.

Chapter Six

I sat at a table trying to ignore the banging in my head, telling myself I was too young to be that hungover. When I stared down at the table and took deep breaths, I began to feel fine, I would then look up and the room would tilt a little and remind me I am not too young at all and that my days of binge drinking will be limited to special occasions.

I used 5% of my phone battery blocking my credit and debit cards, although anyone who did try spending on them would be very disappointed at how little they could purchase before it was declined for insufficient funds. I flicked my phone into airplane mode just to preserve the remaining 5% battery. I did not foresee any drama on the walk home, but such is the way of the modern world, I would feel a sense of vulnerability if my phone died while I had no access to a charger.

A barista was clearing a table at the other side of the coffee shop, and she must have turned too quickly or slipped perhaps, but disaster struck, and a glass mug slipped from the tray and smashed on the floor. The glass mug seemed to shatter excessively. I reckon if I had stuck all that glass back together, I would have been able to make two mugs. Now, I was too hungover to oblige the customary 'whhheeeeyyyyy' when someone in such a position drops something, but it did draw my attention to a gorgeous lady stood in line waiting at the till.

She was looking up at the coffee menu and tapping her chin while thinking, clearly, she was unaware I was staring at her as she quickly picked something out of her teeth, it was adorable. She still has this reaction from me to this day; that I can't believe how beautiful she is, and I just gawk at her and fail miserably at taking it all in, hard as I may try. As cliché as it sounds, she truly took my breath away.

I quickly darted into the toilet; my fellow clientele would have thought I had a stomach upset but my rationale was purely vanity. In the toilet I splashed my face with cold water (from the sink) and began to forensically detail every flaw on my face until I was fully satisfied, she would not look at me twice. I then attempted to smarten myself up, the aftershave I wore last night was cheap and overpowering but it had now faded somewhat and was masking any odours my hungover body was secreting. I smartened myself up as best as I could so that I looked more like a stressed-out overworked banker that had slept in office, and less like, well, you know, a guy that got pissed, threw up, and slept on a park bench. I then returned to my table, I had about 2 mouthfuls of coffee left so if I was going to approach this goddess, I needed a plan and fast.

Check 1, no engagement ring, no wedding ring, this doesn't mean she is single, but there's no visual representation of a commitment. I also can't assume she wants a partner, some people like being alone. Check 2, I still look like shit and have no chance, why am I doing this to myself?! I can't even offer to buy her a drink, the bastard coffee I had cost £3.80!

Life is weird. I was sat there having an absolute meltdown over a complete stranger, who, for some reason I real felt like I needed to ask on a date, and she is just sat gently sipping her…the heck is that? some variation of fruit tea, I think? blissfully unaware that I am even here or having these panic attacks over her. At this point I am telling myself that I am an idiot and needed to just get home and fast, it was a wild night that descended into a peculiar start to a new day, and this sudden obsession will not mix well with my dehydrated brain. I took the last mouthful of coffee and stood up so quickly I needed a second to find my balance and began to walk towards the exit.

There was a fleeting second that we made eye contact, by the time I raise a little smile in her direction she had looked away. Her table was positioned perfectly between the recycling bin and the exit, the anxiety of these next 5 steps were not befitting to such a small task, but my body is reacting as if I was being chased by a stampeding herd of pacificus mastodons. I drew up some courage from remembering what a drunk stranger told me in the smoking yard the night before 'I'm the greatest guy he has ever met, and he would die for me', well, drunk, smoker guy of whom I bonded with very quickly due to alcohol…these next few steps are for the both of us. I can make it. Just a few steps, walk past her and out the door without doing something stupid.

As I strode past, she turned to me and said, "got time?", I was shocked but figured all my staring and, if I'm being honest, bizarre behaviour, was likely to have put the signal out that I am into her. I smiled and said "sure". I pulled out the chair opposite her and sat down. She spoke again, "well?" this took me by surprise, as blunt and short as it was, I didn't really understand the question. Does she just want me to go for it, is she saying well? Are you going to ask me out or?, I needed time to think so I replied with a safe yet unremarkable "well, indeed". She simply tutted and said, "do you have the time?". Oh fuck. Sorry drunk smoking guy, I have failed us. I stammered, "sorry, you want the time", I looked at my wrist, of course, my watch is gone, either lost or stolen.

"Um, no, I don't have the time".

"Right…so, um, why did you sit down?"

"I thought you said, got time? Like you wanted to talk or something."

"But I don't know you! Wouldn't that be weird?"

"I guess so, yes". I reached a point of calm, I had messed this up, I don't feel like it could get worse. May as well go for broke. Seems the stag do had turned me into quite the gambler

Chapter Seven

Where the fuck is she?!

Anxiety has capsized any of the positive thinking I could muster, and I am now swimming against the current in an ocean of despair. My wife has been missing for 12 hours. My fucking wife is missing! This is mental, I do not have any kind of skill set to deal with this. If anything, I am amongst the pool of people this should not happen to due to their lack of coping ability.

I rang the police as soon as the baby and I returned to the B&B, they reckoned, at the time of the call, that 45 minutes didn't count as 'missing' but they did try to calm me down. And this is what my life had come to, being told to calm down by a public body that seems to hire a lot of racists and rapists, and the expectation now is that I take comfort from their words and accept that I was a bit keen with the missing person's call.

The police said that they noted my concern, but it would be a bit premature to send out a search party. They took some further details from me so that if I call back in a few hours, they can begin their investigation which I already know is going to be the case. I am desperate for them to just crack on and make sure my wife is safe, so I stressed every detail I could and asked for confirmation that it had been noted down.

While I don't fully trust them, they are all I have. It shouldn't need further clarity that I know my wife very well. Is this the first time she has gone off ahead without looking back? No, is this the first time she has done that, and I have not been able to find her? Yes. And that is why I am so scared and anxious. There is something off, and everything just feels different. She always said I had a talent for appearing wherever she was, as of today I have to admit that talent has been retired.

The baby has slept soundly which I am both thankful and amazed by. Amazed because I must be radiating negativity and fear, yet the youngest soul in the room exhibits nothing but tranquillity. I'm thankful because I feel like my whole body is humming, if I laid on the table now, I would just end up on the floor on my back still ticking over slightly like an old wind-up toy soldier. I tried sleeping, but for obvious reasons I couldn't. And had it not been for the little one I wouldn't have even been back to the room, I would be out there, looking relentlessly.

I needed to call my parents. I did not want to, but I need them to look after the baby while I am searching for Lainya. I can't be a panic-stricken husband and competent father, not even your most experienced circus clown could display such a juggling act. I needed them to come here, but not interfere, I needed them to step up but not ask questions. Asking them to come over to Melas no questions asked is a big ask. How do I even word this?

The phone begins to ring, my hands shaking like a compulsive masturbater, my mum answers, as soon as I hear her voice I want to break down in tears and ask for a hug, I bite my lip until I feel frustrated with myself then speak "Mum, I need you and dad to come here and babysit please, I will pay for your tickets, your accommodation everything, but we have got some unexpected work to do here and I really need your help".

I knew if I told her the 'work' was a missing persons mission that just so happened to be someone who is front and centre of the family there would be a justifiable widespread panic. I needed my parents to be calm and blissfully unaware, so that pumpkin can have the care and attention she deserves. Also, Dad has a dodgy heart, and I am almost certain such a level of drama would kill him, and selfishly I just do not need that right now. Somewhat ironic that his ticker is a timebomb.

While my daughter is sleeping soundly in her travel cot, I decided to go down to the reception quickly and see if they had another family room I could book for my Mum and Dad so they could stay with us. It felt unnerving leaving the room, with everything that is going on I needed the familiarity as a comfort and being away from the little one, especially now seemed so wrong. While it is a room, I am panicking in it isn't a panic room, though I've just realised I felt safe in it. I checked the balcony door was locked, more times than I care to admit, I doubled checked every window in the room and was able to confirm with myself that I would be able to leave the room for a few minutes without my baby being in danger. Baby monitor in hand I started to approach the reception. I then double back to check our room door was locked.

This was all further proof that my life must be a sitcom for some extra-terrestrial comedy channel for a faraway galaxy of alien beings because while taking comfort from my room and its familiarity, the whole of the downstairs area had been renovated and completely changed since yesterday, and I'll be honest, I think it sucks. Too modern, no charm, just smooth white walls, and a tiled floor with grey rugs which I assume is faux fur. I approached the reception area which also had some new features, such as a touch screen monitor for people to enter their car registration, that wasn't there yesterday. In fact, I must say, they do not mess around here on this island, the last 12 hours have been a blur, but whichever renovation team worked on this put in an impressive no-nonsense shift. This kind of renovation job would have taken months to complete back home. It is almost unbelievable. If it hadn't been for the fact I had just left my room, I would assume I had entered the wrong B&B.

There were two young ladies on the desk this time with a matching uniform and a scripted approach to the clientele. While teetering on the edge of pure depression I had not lost my ability for small talk and fake enthusiasm. "Place looks great, real out with the old in with the new kind of vibe, I love it" I hated it, I lied. The two receptionists looked at each other and then looked back at me, a hint of concern in their eyes and then got down to business "are you okay sir?" I guess news travels fast and for now, I am going to be the guy with the missing wife.

It wasn't something I wished to discuss right now, it is not something I think I could discuss without crying so I cut to the chase and enquired about a room for my folks to which I was told there was only one room left but it was a single bed and could not accommodate a travel cot. I assume the reception staff could sense my frustration, or they felt sorry for me, but either way they were very helpful and kindly made some recommendations to other local hotels and

B&Bs. They allowed me to use the phone on their reception so I wouldn't have to walk around to the other places.

I managed to book my parents in at a hotel just 2 miles from here in a generous sized room, I mean, it was a honeymoon suite with a heart shaped bed and inappropriately placed hot tub, but it was a large room and that's what they deserved for helping us out like this. I gave the phone back to the receptionist and smiled just as the baby monitor made a noise to tell me sleeping beauty was beginning to stir.

I turned to walk back to the room, but froze when I looked at the baby monitor, I felt winded and dizzy, there was a cloaked figure standing over my daughter's cot, motionless but apparently staring with some form of intent. My blood ran cold, and knees went weak, by the time the shiver had reached my toes I had clicked into Dad mode and began sprinting to our room.

Chapter Eight

I don't know if my heart was racing or if it was trying to burst out of my chest to give me something to throw at this intruder that is standing over my baby. I reached my door in remarkable time, my inhaling and exhaling not aligning to what could be considered as breathing properly. I was in pure panic mode, needing to get into our room but confused as to how someone had gotten in there. The only possible way, and it is quite a scary thought, is that this cloaked person had been in our room undetected the entire time, just waiting for me to leave.

I put the card up to the door handle to unlock it, it flashed red and made a grinding noise to let me know the key was declined, I glanced up at the door, number 9, this is my room, I tried again, the adrenaline pumping through my system made coordination seem an underappreciated luxury of the past, now I was just shaking in a general direction and hoping for the best. Same grinding noise, same red flashes as if looking into the eyes of lucifer. I took a step back, right, drastic measures time, I booted the door as hard as I could, I quickly doubled over in pain and fell to the floor clutching my ankle, my foot seemed to bend inwards like a rubber sole as soon as it struck the MDF. I knew I had to jump up and do it again, my daughter is in danger, and I don't care if my shin bone snaps and protrudes through my foot by the time I get in there.

As I stood up and fumbled for my card key, I had the realisation that during my panicked state I had been using my credit card rather than room card to get entry into my room, no time to curse myself out, I switched cards and put it to the handle, green, I'm in. I ran into the entrance, past the small pokey bathroom and threw my hands up to fight.

My arms fell limply by my side as I looked at my dressing gown hanging helplessly in front of the cot. I dropped helplessly to my knees, I buried my head into my hands, half relieved that I wasn't having to fight someone, and half embarrassed by what had transpired.

Ugghhhh, it was my dressing gown. What the fuck is wrong with me. Life with anxiety does not get any easier. It is probably amusing for those around me, but I am not in the mood. I nearly kicked a door down to protect my daughter from my dressing gown. Well, actually, I nearly broke my ankle while trying to save my daughter from nothing. Life has ways of being cruel at the most undeserving of times, sleep deprived, stressed, anxious, missing wife, and then to top it off, your mind starts playing tricks on you.

It might be early in the morning, but I am going to call it and write it off already…today can fuck off.

I started making a coffee, more out of habit than need, all thing's considered caffeine is not a requirement for me currently, in fact all things considered a coffee right now is a terrible idea, but I needed to be doing something to keep my mind occupied. I flicked on the TV and sat at the foot of my bed and watched the local news. I was half expecting and hoping for some form of 'news just in, missing woman' special, but there was no mention of Lainya, just news that the pier had reopened, the local deli now boasts 14 different flavours of ice cream followed by an agonising sequence of vox pops asking locals which their favourite flavour of the new selection is, and news that some strange lights had been spotted around the lighthouse in the last week but authorities say there is nothing to be concerned about. For me, the news was saying a lot while saying absolutely nothing important at all.

I called the reception of the hotel that my parents would be staying at using the room phone and requested that they emailed my parents the confirmation of their accommodation and other details of their stay. I also used the phone to arrange their travel and asked for these details to be sent also, as my mobile phone had no signal, no internet and was thusly redundant. Finally, I politely requested that they ended their email to my parents with an agreed time that I would drop off little one with them.

I did not want any mention of Lainya in this message or what my 'work' was once they had arrived so it was helpful that the reception staff at their hotel would email them. I am too tired and too stressed that I feel like if I typed a message, it would either have an undertone that would encourage further questions or just be nonsensical and I would end up with missing parents as well as a missing spouse. I don't know how I'm going to keep myself together when I do see my mum, because lord knows I am so scared.

Right now, I need to stay positive and not give off too much off a negative vibe around the baby, I don't know how much little ones pick up on this stuff or how damaging it is, if at all, but I do not want to take any risks. Once she is awake, we will get dressed and head on out, I will let the police know how they can reach me, but I sense they think I am overreacting anyway. Despite myself I may take little one down to the deli and let her try some of this famous ice cream that was so newsworthy. I might even tell her the tall tale of the phantom dressing gown that she was nearly gobbled up by.

I really do wish Lainya was here, I need her, she would know how to best deal with this situation. Although having her here to deal with her not being here would somewhat make the situation redundant.

I don't know what I am doing.

Chapter Nine

I can confirm that the old saying 'opposites attract' applies to Lainya and I. We only have the bare minimum in common, we both like music but I love hip-hop, she loves drum n bass. We both like reading, but she likes horror as a genre whereas I like autobiographies. My favourite takeaway is Pizza, hers is Chinese. But our differences made for good conversation, we made it work for us. Annoying habits is another thing, Lainya's most annoying habit is always moving the phone charger and not returning it. My most annoying habit is I occasionally tend to rhyme the last few words she says to me, doubly annoying because I'm not a particularly skilled rapper. It's a nervous habit, I'm working on it.

In the early stages of our relationship, Lainya definitely played hard to get, but to be honest I kind of liked that, being aware that she was significantly out of my league it made sense to me that I would need to prove myself and pull out all the stops to show I was worthy. We can safely assume I did not go into it with high self-esteem and confidence, so either of those opposing qualities would not have been characteristics of mine she found endearing.

Having failed to give her the time when we first met, I was lucky to fall back on my greatest gift, autopilot small talk.

"So do you come here often?"

"Yes, every morning before work"

"Ah, so you have a job?"

"Yes, and that reaction seems a little sexist".

"Oh, no, oh dear, god no, not sexist, I think what I meant was, what do you do for a job?"

"That's not what you said though?!"

"No, it isn't it. Look, I am really sorry, can we try that again?"

She looked at me for what seemed to be an age, it felt very intense and in my mind our entire future, if I can call it that, rested on how she responded to that question. She let out a sigh, which startled me slightly as I had started staring at her beauty and then this gorgeous half smile appeared, and she said, "Let's talk about you".

"So, you are wearing a pretty nice suit, although it clearly needs a good iron. Do you come here every day too?"

I am going to now I thought to myself, plus I thought my suit looked okay, but what I said to her was "most mornings yeah, get that caffeine fix for the day ahead" I pumped a hearty fist while saying this and hated myself immediately. I was taking two steps forward with the autopilot small talk and one step backwards with the accompanying body language.

"And what is it you do for a living?"

Now it did not seem impressive to tell her I was on long term sickness leave with anxiety or that the sickness leave I was on was from a telecom company. I was not ashamed to be on sickness leave, one's mental health should always be a priority and I will happily champion that, however, context is always important and at this stage of this current conversation it did not sound impressive. I could mention I have my own business buying cheap protein bars in bulk and selling them on. Alas, a little probing and quick internet search would reveal the company went bust after 6 months and I am still paying rent for an empty warehouse because I am too nervous to call the landlord. So, what I said was:

"I work in data analysis".

Her eyes lit up. Which was all the encouragement I needed.

"Yeah, I'm always in the office with graphs and shit, analysing the data with bar charts and PowerPoints".

She looked less impressed.

I said, "Sorry, what is it you do?"

"I work in data analysis; I have never used a bar chart for my findings though".

Well would you believe it? For fucks sake why?!

"Ah brilliant" I lie, "we have that in common then, we can probably talk for hours about data and our favourite ways to interpret it, and numbers and stuff?"

"I would really rather not"

Oh, thank God. That could have ended very badly. I am such an Idiot.

We had a little more chatter and then left it there, she had to get to work, and I had to walk home and sleep on something more comfortable than a bench, and then treat myself to a shower. All in all, that felt like a success with just a small sprinkling, perhaps a seasoning, of disaster.

The next day I showed up at the café. I sat at the same table as the one that had transformed into a throne for a Queen the day before and had my cup of coffee and a fruity tea for my dream lady sat opposite, I figured this was the best way to integrate the chance meeting into a smooth casual together, all I need to do was smile as she entered and simply motion towards the tea, take it or leave it, not too forward, not too strong, and hopefully it comes across as rather sweet.

She didn't show. That was a Tuesday. Wednesday, no show, Thursday no show. So Friday was the day, I told myself if she didn't show up then I would give up, especially considering how the barista looked at me on the Thursday as I ordered my two drinks and positioned them perpendicularly on the table and sat staring into the abyss for 40 minutes before picking up what would have been her mug and asking for its contents to be transferred into a takeout cup, for the third day in a row. I was transitioning from keen to sad to just outright pathetic.

Friday happened, she strolled through the door brilliant sunshine beaming behind her as she entered, birds removing her jacket and letting it float effortlessly to her chair opposite me, angels singing, as she took each step in slow motion. That is how it should have happened anyway.

"Oh hello"

"Your morning beverage awaits you miss" I said, sounding like an utter twat.

"How did you know I would be here?"

"You said you came here each morning before work" I said, somehow sounding like a bigger twat.

"Right, well I have been in London for a work conference the last few days, so as you can imagine it is quite the coincidence you are here today".

"Indeed" I said, knowing that she thinks I'm a total weirdo stalker "Coincidence, fate, I don't think we need to label it" it was at that moment the Barista walked past and slapped me the back encouragingly "ah, she's finally shown up eh, 4th times the charm" I completely ignored that had been said and just smiled at her. She had a look on her face that I couldn't quite read, she was either blushing and excited about where this was heading or was mortified and wished she was dead.

If there is one area we did not quite complement each other at this stage it was her lack of small talk or engagement with me, but the way she looked at me told me she was at the very least intrigued by me, and at the most outlandish, into me.

"Well thank you for the drink, really, but I have to get to work".

"Sure, me too" I lied, the only thing on my agenda was to go home and sob. "Hey, before you go, are you single?"

"Maybe"

That's a yes." same again Monday?"

"Maybe"

That's an annoying response. "Can I have your number?"

"No, not right now"

"Oh, well, Monday then?"

"We will see won't we, have a nice weekend".

And off she went. I was a mixture of confused, pissed off, and excited. And to be feeling all those things at once it must be love.

Chapter Ten

Recognising I'm in a heightened emotional state I am consciencely making the effort to not argue with, or snap at anyone, but this 14-flavour ice cream bragging is overly generous to what they are serving. The most adventurous flavour on offer is rum & raisin which is pretty standard at all ice cream outlets. The reason I say generous is because they have selections like strawberry, and then next to that 'double strawberry' or chocolate, double chocolate, triple chocolate, and what seems to be the ultimate cop out, extra creamy vanilla, next to vanilla. So that's 8 of the 14 and it's really just vanilla, strawberry, chocolate varieties.

"One scoop of strawberry in a carton please"

"Right away sir, now is that strawberry, or double strawberry?"

"Just a single scoop of single strawberry please"

"Okay sir, we also have a strawberry and cream flavour ice cream as part of our 14-flavour relaunch".

"Impressive" I say sarcastically. We then stand across from each other in silence, this interaction has already gone beyond tedious and is entering frustrating, I feel prepared to smash his face into his 14-flavour cart, in fact I will make smashing his face in a double, maybe a triple.

"So? Can I interest you in the strawberries and Cream flavour?"

"No, mate come on! Please do not make me ask a third time for a scoop of SINGLE STRAWBERRY!"

"No need to be rude, Jesus, you need to chill, here".

As we exchanged ice cream for Money, and he turned to get my change I found peace with the image of him struggling to pull along his cart with the handle shoved up his arse. I grabbed a little plastic spoon and pushed the pram towards the harbour wall where we could sit in the shade. 'You need to chill' I wonder if that was an intended pun?

I am now wondering if leaving the B&B was a good idea, every woman with blonde hair makes my heart skip a beat thinking for a split second that I have found my wife. Maybe she has fell and hit her head and is strolling around the island confused and lost. I guess if I had stayed in that room with the phantom dressing gown, I would have gone crazy, but it just feels so wrong to not be out there searching frantically. I know I have a responsibility to look after the baby, at least until my parents arrive in the morning.

Every little detail is causing me to feel conflicted, the scenery is beautiful no doubt, but a couple of times a drone has gone whizzing by my head like a mechanical insect, and I can still hear the faint buzzing they give off, manmade pests, mind you there is a hell of a lot of them. It makes it hard to be present. I am here with my baby, and I should be forever grateful for that, but I just can't help being frustrated that 99% of the ice cream has come out of her mouth and rolled down her chin so it has proved to be a waste of money in both ice cream and baby wipes. I am on an island, renowned for its unique craft beer, but this is not the time for me to indulge, and finally, this is meant to be time with my wife, for us all together as a family, and guess what, she is actually missing! I literally have no idea where she is?!

I look down at the floor and let out a big sigh, a tear rolls down my cheek, this is all so messed up. I wipe my tear away and look up at my daughter and smile I say, "we're going to be fine pumpkin, you'll see. Don't worry about a thing". I look down at the floor again and doubt floods my brain and spills out into my soul, and I look back at her "I'm so sorry I'm the one you have to rely on".

I then pull the collar of my t-shirt over my eyes so my daughter can't see me desperately sobbing.

Chapter Eleven

I was almost celebrated by my friends for how I was able to secure a date after what seemed like a disastrous debacle of a first meeting, not to mention the couple of follow up coffee shop rendezvous that were kind of awkward at best. Furthermore, she is way out of my league, something I mention a lot, not as a brag but more that I cannot believe my own luck. Taking all this into account I should not have to buy my own pint ever again, I am a champion.

The other times we met for coffee and, classing it as meeting is a bit of a stretch admittedly, was not a great success, but it was progressive, she knows my name now, she does smile when she sees me, and she genuinely thinks I am in there getting a coffee before work. It is not quite a masterplan, in fact, it is not even a plan, I am just acting on instinct, but I think she is starting to like me, or she likes getting a free cuppa every morning. I told myself to not show up one day and see if that makes her think about me a bit more, but it all seemed a bit manipulative, and I felt I was becoming my own red flag. Whatever I was, I was, as always, in my own head too much.

This particular morning, I remember as it was special to our lives, having got there early and asking the barista for "the usual" she came in slightly later than normally expected 13 minutes to be exact, but who's counting? I was. She seemed a bit flustered, she said her alarm hadn't gone off, or it had gone off and she fell straight back to sleep without realising. Either way, she has had a mad rush to get ready for her morning cup of tea and feels ugly. The takeaways from that being that she said she wasn't late for work, she said was late for tea, she wants to see me! And she also fished for a compliment and knows I'm 'that guy', "nonsense, you look perfect! Come on, first time we met I bet you thought I had slept on a bench or something and crawled into the café", she laughed and then threw her work bag down, and excused herself for the toilet.

What made this such a turning point and big occasion for me, and subsequently us, was that as her bag was put down a few of her work belongings spilled out, pen, diary, fob, and business cards, I know now where she works, the company of which she analyses the data. This was an opening for romantic gestures to begin pouring in, nothing too crazy or over the top, just a gesture to let her know I think about her. I am very aware that I am thinking all this to myself and how weird it sounds, but in a world of dating moving swiftly into the digital age, some old school romance could work in my favour.

Upon returning from the toilet, she explained she hadn't slept well, and informed me she is having a reoccurring nightmare which is keeping her awake. She then tried to brush that off as childish, but I encouraged her to tell me more, it was brilliant, she was confiding in me. I mean, obviously she was dealing with something and that was sad to know, but that did not detract away from her opening up, and to me, the ultimate deep-thinking empath. Time. To. Connect.

As much as she tried to brush it off as childish nonsense, I made it a safe space for discussion, non-judgmental, and if I'm being honest, she had me hooked. She explained that it freaks her out so much because she dreamt of these people plotting awful things in a cave, there is stuff like gruesome art on the cave walls from smeared blood and gutted animals laying discarded on the floor. Then, in the dream the people all stop suddenly and turn from their huddle and point to where she is standing. With that she has the realisation she is in the cave with them and one of them says in a truly dreadful growl 'Lainya'.

"Good God"

"I know, it's stupid".

"No Lainya, it is not stupid. I mean that sounds scary, I would be freaked out. And you say this is happening a lot?"

"Three times this week"

"it's Tuesday today so you either had a nap as well, or you count Sunday as the start of the week".

"That's your takeaway from this?"

"No, sorry, of course not. It must be frightening having a dream like that, and reoccurring, there must be some kind of meaning, but what?"

"I don't know, but when I initially wake up, I just feel so creeped out, and then during the day I just feel stupid that it has upset me so much".

"Lainya, it's not stupid at all".

"It doesn't even make any sense?!"

"I think the fact it's reoccurring, and it ends with them pointing and saying your name, uggh, it is creepy. What are you going to do?"

"Go to work! Thanks for the drink".

That moment when it ended really sucked, I remember asking myself why do people have jobs, that conversation had so much more milage in it and that is definitely the most personal we had gotten on our non-random coffee non-dates, dates. I decided to go for a walk around the local park as I needed to have a debrief with myself and unpack everything I had learnt. I had been given a lot of information that morning for my conquest, I felt like this was time to act, but was not sure what I should do?

Chapter Twelve

She left her work building at 5.15 pm and looked shocked, sick, confused and then cautiously happy at the sight of me stood at the other side of the road with a bunch of flowers. She said bye to a couple of her colleagues and then came over to me.

"Erm, hello?"

"Oh hi, well this is awkward, I'm here waiting for a date".

"Funny"

"I was going for playful. Look, I'm not a psychologist, I don't know what your dreams mean but my dream is quite simple, let me take you on a date". That line was only partially scripted, but I nailed it.

She looked at me, either overcome with such a romantic gesture, or wondering how every decision she had made in life had led her to this moment. I slowly started to go from confident to feeling like I may have struck out and this wasn't going to happen. I took a step back and held out the flowers, a goodbye gesture, it had meant a lot to me, but the coffee train ends here my love. She laughed and pulled her lush shiny hair from out of its professional bobble and let it drop below her shoulders.

"Come on, I know a great place to eat just around the corner".

Jackpot.

And that is how our first date happened.

Chapter Thirteen

I felt I was in a strange predicament, I have been desperate for my parents to get here so I could drop off pumpkin with people that I can trust, but at the same time I feel an anxiety of entering the next phase of whatever it is I was in. The little one has been the main focus of my attention throughout this, and once she has been dropped off, I really have to face this. Three days, no contact, no sightings. I have to admit that something is really, really wrong.

I made my way across the Island to where my parents' accommodation was, I had received a notification from the reception staff at my B&B of a message from my mum letting me know they had arrived, 'safely' as well. Nice additional, yet not really required, detail. I imagine anything more sinister would warrant a phone call rather than a 'pass it on' message, 'Hi, arrived safe, your father lost an arm, lots of blood, hope to see you soon' that wouldn't work. There is still no signal on my mobile phone which is becoming a growing frustration.

I am psyching myself up to try and remain composed for this interaction, despite being a grown man there is something about seeing my mum when I feel vulnerable that reverts me back to the toddler stage of development and I just want a cuddle while I cry and seek assurance that everything will be okay. Even if I am feeling poorly at home, I just want my mum to come and care for me, not that I would ever ask that of her.

I reached my parents door and took a deep breath, this is it, you have two things to be, cool, and calm, you can do this. I knock.

"Oh my god what's wrong?"

"What? Nothing?"

"Don't lie to me, I know when something is wrong with my boy".

"Mum is this really any way to answer the door".

"Sorry, come on in, and then tell me what's wrong".

"Nothing is wrong"

"Where's Lainya?"

"Working, I'm going to go and join her as soon as I've unpacked this case".

"I can do that, don't you worry. Do you want a coffee?"

"No thank you".

"HA! see, there is something wrong, you always reject a coffee if your anxiety is playing up".

"It could be that Mum, or it could be that I had one literally 5 minutes ago, Mum everything is fine, it is a bit of a nuisance that we have to do some work on this holiday but look, I am fine. Thank you so much for looking after the little one, and please enjoy yourselves. Whatever you spend

I will reimburse you, you are doing us a huge favour. Now I have really got to go" I give her a kiss on the cheek "Love you", Kiss the baby "Love you, be good" and finally shouting towards the balcony which I also quickly scanned was baby proof "Love you Dad". He didn't turn around he was too busy watching boats, he just lifted a hand as if to wave bye and left it there, cool as they come.

I walked down their corridor and out the building and instantly felt cut off and lonely, I had tears rolling down my cheeks and I was gnawing the inside of my mouth to avoid me fully breaking into tears, I realised with all this happening along with my blank stare made me look like I was probably under the influence of drugs, and this was confirmed by the amount of people moving out of my way.

I need to think of a plan now to find my wife, I lack all the ingredients that would make a good detective, and on top of that I have an absurd low level of common sense, hence why she is generally the decision maker in the marriage. I am merely the labrador, loyal and happy to do whatever, just happy to be involved. It was an odd feeling, but I was starting to feel a bit angry towards Lainya, she's missing, I have subsequently completely fell apart, the holiday is ruined, my parents have had to come out here, the baby is with them, all because she had to rush ahead and see the fucking sea first?! Why couldn't she have just walked with us, why did she have to rush ahead?

I strolled back to my accommodation and as soon as I entered the reception staff beckoned me over, oh God please tell me Lainya has been found and is in our room, please God please, I would never question your existence ever again, I promise I will join whichever religion is truly yours. I reached the reception. "The police are here, and they are in your room,".

"Why are they in my room?"

"To speak to you".

"And you just let them in my room?"

"Yes"

"Right, I don't think you are picking up on my annoyance, why did you let them in my personal space?"

"Do you not want to speak with them?"

"Yes, but…It just seems odd that they are in my room with my stuff, it's fine, I am glad they're here".

"Okay sir"

"Was it you that let them in?"

"Yes sir, just 5 minutes after you left with the pram".

"Okay great, rather it be you than my fisherman friend, do you usher him into the staff room when the police turn up?"

"Sir?"

"The fisherman guy who checked us in when we arrived" I pointed to the photo on the wall, "him there" there was a look of confusion on the receptionist's face, she looked like she was going to speak and then stopped herself, she then looked at the photo I was still pointing to and said "Sir, you must be mistaken". I scoffed, not insulted by the notion but self-righteous in my certainty "No, I am not mistaken", I then pointed at him again, this time tapping the glass, "this gentleman here booked me in at the start of our stay, it was a very memorable encounter".

"Sir, that photo is over 200 years old, everyone in it has been dead a long time".

Chapter Fourteen

It transpired that I did not have to go to my room to speak to the police, they came to me to 'escort' me away from the reception. I had become slightly agitated and lashed out, not physically of course, not particularly verbally either, but I can assume I acted in a way that may have concerned the reception staff. I will make sure I apologise later, that is not who I am…But still, what the hell. Missing wife? Check. Police here to see me? Check. Surely those two things would deter someone from taking the piss out of me, I am clearly a man on the edge. "He's been dead 200 years" good one! I am still fuming. In different circumstances I would have probably enjoyed it, but not now.

I was accompanied into a private function room, it doesn't look like there will be any events here any time soon, the stage area was thick with dust and the wings had a disgusting looking red velvet curtain with a gold trim. Tables and chairs are spread about as if everyone had left in a hurry, there is a speaker in the corner just recklessly left on its side with half its frame splintered and chipped away, and on top of it is a broken wine glass. It is like karaoke for the dammed. The paint on the ceiling was flaking away and showing signs of damp, and this was not consistent with my experience of this place thus far. It seemed almost abandoned. If anything had died 200 years ago it was this room. There is a rune, or possibly a sigil etched in the wooden headrests on each chair, it could just be a basic foreign symbol to be fair, I am not a well-travelled man, but it does draw the eye. It is an upside-down triangle with what seems to be an anchor protruding through it and the centre of the anchor has a moon etched into it. I assume it must be a nod the Islands, proud fishing heritage.

I glance over at the two police pulling out a couple of chairs and dusting their seats with a handkerchief before sitting, one of them looked bewildered by the unkept nature of the room, the other looked nervous. I lacked the elegance they, somewhat literally, brought to the table, and just gave my chair a quick wipe with my sleeve before sitting down. I looked at them expecting they would get the conversation started, they are the professionals after all, however, they just stared at me, clearly with an expectation I was not familiar with.

It was equal parts awkward, and unsettling. It was made doubly awkward because when the lights were turned on in here it must have also switched on the disco ball which has just slowly started spinning and giving the impression that the three of us are at a High School reunion.

I thought I would get started with proceedings, "Look, I am sorry about the reception just now".

The policeman stuck out his bottom lip and waved his hand to let me know it is not an issue or requires any further discussion, they both then continued to stare at me. I guess in a missing persons enquiry the spouse is the first suspect.

It is a bizarre feeling knowing I need their help desperately but also being aware I am a suspect, and they will be applying a meticulous scrutiny to my words.

The older Policeman of the two began to talk, "Right then, introductions I am Detective North, and this here is my partner, Detective Tim Rooker. And you are…" his partner interrupts "the hysterical guy from the reception!" Detective North and I just stare at him, I think he was trying to be funny, maybe lighten the mood, idiot. "I was going to say, and you are Nathan, so Nathen tell us about your wife".

"Sure, we met…" I was once again met with the lower lip and handwave combo.

"How has she ended up missing?"

"We were by the beach, she was walking ahead, she likes to lead, I was struggling to keep up because I was dragging the pram through soft sand so there was no traction, and once I got to the beach she was gone. I double backed, looked on the sand dunes, found her footwear but could not see her anywhere. I shouted her name for ages, I then reluctantly came back here so that I could call you guys and report it".

"Yes, she had not been missing for long when you called us".

"Forgive me, just the fact she was 'missing' was a cause for concern" I said this hoping my anger wasn't obvious to them, I hoped that the subtle sarcasm masked the frustration at their clear lack of engagement with this.

"Do you have a photo of your wife"

"Of course," I presented them with my phone.

"These seem to be from quite a distance".

"You can zoom in, that's her. Like I say she is the leader of the family"

"And this?"

"That! That is our daughter, she's with my parents at the minute".

The Detectives looked to each other, nodded, and simply said "We will be in touch".

"What happens now?"

"You wait, and please, I know this is easier said than done but try not to panic".

I sat and watched them leave, biting my lower lip, biting the insides of my mouth, stopping myself shouting some dumb shit at them which would only make me feel better momentarily but worse in the long run. I laid my head on the table hoping I could close my eyes and gather my thoughts; however, the tablecloth stank so I quickly abandoned that idea and left the room with haste.

I passed the reception, and they gave me an apologetic smile, I felt a sense of sympathy radiating from them. I walked over to the desk, "I am so sorry about before, you were probably just trying to build some rapport with your customer. I guess I'm just a little stressed and tired and don't have much of a sense of humour right now. Forgive me". They nodded and smiled awkwardly. I went back to my room hoping I would get some form of inspiration. I paced back and forth but had no light bulb moment so I figured I would head back to the beach, the spot she went missing, hopefully I might find something that will help me find her.

Chapter Fifteen

We had been dating a short while; I do not recall exactly how long, and I find that detail irrelevant. For me, it was about the feeling I got when I was with her rather than how many hours of her time I could capture, feelings should not be undermined or determined by time. It was not plain sailing for me, far from it, but I maintain that it is rare that something special is easy to obtain, you must put in work, at least, that is my understanding of the universe. I am however, far from an expert and would sooner advise someone ignore my romantic advice than aspire toward it.

There was a lot of uncertainty in the early stages of the relationship, and while it did wonders for my coffee shop rewards card, it was of detriment to my health, and I really struggled with the anxiety of arranging to see her again and wondering if she liked me or not. We had times that while we were together, she seemed distant, we would go to eat together but she would walk in front of me to the restaurant, I sometimes wondered if she was ashamed to be seen with me.

My thoughts proved to be complete nonsense, just my anxiety trying to trip me up, my poor mental health trying to cast shade on a beautiful moment. I do wish I had been better with 'banter' though she would tell me that since we met, she hasn't been able to "get rid of me". I would just smile desperately trying to think of something witty to retort with, a flirtatious lightbulb would eventually illuminate but by then the moment had passed.

Being a lifelong partner to poor mental health I knew ways to suppress the uncertainty and keep myself calm, and one method was to shower her quite simply with love, which meant I stopped thinking about me and put my energy into her. She had certainly improved my life, I was becoming, if I do say so myself, a better person. I got a part time job working in a library, my knowledge of self-help books was wildly redundant, but I did enjoy the escapism of just casually putting books on a shelf in a quiet environment. I tried some DIY, but my homemade bird table turned into a rather gruesome deathtrap for our winged friends, so I expertly transformed it into firewood to prevent any further deaths. The majority of my wages went on flowers, chocolate, and wine, generic maybe but if you look at these gift websites there is very little else on offer.

I decided the best way to get rid of the uncertainty and reduce my anxiety was to ask her to marry me. It signalled my intent and showed her, and everyone else, how serious I was about her, the response to me would give me an indication of how much I needed to worry. If she said 'yes' it would have meant I could relax and enjoy life with my dream women. A 'no' meant I would have been right to be crippled with worry and constant, never ending, excruciating stress. A 'maybe' would mean a change in my diet to anti-depressants seasoned with painkillers for breakfast, dinner, and tea, maybe even supper.

My friends, my parents, my new work colleagues all thought I was crazy. Too soon. My ever-supportive Dad and his few words of wisdom were "leave that poor woman alone". I expected nothing less from the root cause of my anxiety, I love him though. I understood why they were all concerned, for most people this would be far too soon. But how do you explain an emotion or a sense you have to others. I felt it was the right thing to do, it made perfect sense.

While I almost exclusively make bad choices, I did not feel like this is one I would ever regret. Granted, it could have gone wrong, destroyed my life and motivation and I would have ended up living on the streets eating melted cheese from discarded takeaway packaging and sinking the dregs of coffee from takeout cartons. But at least I had a backup plan there, although I dare say my survival skills could have done with some improvements.

Chapter Sixteen

I had heard that an engagement ring should 'traditionally' be the equivalent of 3 months' salary. Call me a cynic but I assumed this 'tradition' had been invented by engagement rings marketing teams. Now, I had a problem here, mainly that I only worked part time in a library, 3 months wages would not afford me anything of real quality. The other problem is the landlord and other bill collectors would not grant me a 3-month grace period for the notion of romance. I would assume that in a corporate world of profit and greed, romance would seem rather childish. And finally, to really garnish the main dish of issues thus completing the trilogy of problems, I can't wait 3 months.

Since I had the idea, I really wanted to crack on with it, I am rather impatient when I am excited about something. Impulsive is probably the best word for it. I have been known to arrive at football games 2 hours before kick-off purely because I am excited and there are no distractions that preoccupy my mind or are big enough, so I would rather just be there and wait for the game to begin.

Secure in the knowledge that all my loved ones thought it was not a great idea, I proceeded and took out a small loan, one that I would gradually be able to financially recover from, but big enough to find a beautiful ring. That, it would seem, was the easy part, now I needed to decide how I was going to propose?! Big romantic gestures were easy to think of, but difficult to afford. I did not want to just take her for a meal and propose to her there, too basic. I thought about picnics on the hilltop when the sun is setting but I think the intimacy and the surroundings would serve as a giveaway and I wanted it to be a big surprise. So, I needed think less like a romantic, and more like a crazy person. Crazy in love is probably the happy medium.

Being besotted with someone means it is easy for you to notice the small details that would help in such circumstances. If you remove the intense vulnerability, I was in a great position. I obviously know where she lives, I knew which hours she works, which route she takes, I even know the window in her kitchen does not lock properly and that if it is lifted as much as the frame permits and rattled a bit it will eventually open. She has never had this fixed because to look at it, it appears closed, and even if you were a chance cat burglar, or...you know, me, it was still very stiff and difficult to open, so fixing it seemed an unnecessary expense. So that was my way in, I was not thrilled by any means at the prospect of essentially 'breaking into' my girlfriends' house but at least I wasn't breaking to enter as such. I doubt anyone has ever been jailed for breaking to marry, and hopefully she won't care anyway when she sees me and the surprise, I have planned for her.

I entered her residence with all the grace one would expect of socially awkward and anxious soul. In fact, it went worse than I thought it would if I am being honest, I managed to encourage the window open with ease. I then reversed into the opening and kicked her bonsai tree off the kitchen side and silently screamed no while I watched it shatter, pottery splinted into spilt soil and broken branches. She loved that tree, she'd had it for years, she would stroke its tiny leaves and call it baby. And I have just murdered it. Little bastard.

I then lowered myself off the kitchen side smashing a gin glass and a coffee cup in the process. My career debut in breaking into properties lived true to the title of the act. I felt absolutely awful, and I promised to myself that I would replace all the things I had broken in the last 15 seconds. Another bit of bad luck was that the window jarred and would not close to its original position. I fought with it for some time, and it barely moved a centimetre. If for some reason she entered from the back after work this would surely arouse suspicion. And this was when I had a panic attack.

After I had calmed down, I got straight to work. I filled each room with tea light candles, they were pretty safe, thus reducing the chances of starting an inferno to accompany my calamitous effort, also, and perhaps more potent, they were cheap. I meticulously colour coordinated them with each room, pink in the bedroom, white in the living room, and orange in the kitchen. I had hoped she would notice this because, to my frustration, I realised that they were scent free, so it did not add to the surprise beyond being nicely coordinated. I had assumed the white would smell like fresh cotton, the pink would be roses, and the orange would be some form of citrus aroma. They were not. They smelt of nothing. It even said scent free on the label, they pride themselves on it. I am an idiot, always rushing, always making tiny errors.

I realised that I was being followed around the house by muddy footprints. I had dragged some of the outdoors, indoors. Further evidence that should I turn to a life of crime, it would not take long for the police to track me down. I removed my trainers and began looking for the dustpan and brush to erase my route around the house. I opened a door to a cupboard I had not been acquainted with before, and as I knelt down to search for a brush of some sort, I noticed a small sliding door which I was sure would either store cleaning utensils, or possibly more shoes. I slid it open and was fairly surprised to see a collection of old books. I took a few out but I was not familiar with the language they were written in. On the basis of the images it was clear these were old fashioned books about some foreign island and strange inhabitants, really cool stuff.

I remember she used to have nightmares about people in caves, and wondered if these books influenced those nightmares, or if the nightmares dictated the purchase of this collection. I wondered if she can actually make sense of these. It would be intriguing if she knew a foreign language. I did not know why she would hide this stuff; it is ace. Maybe the bookcase's modern aesthetic would be disrupted by the presence of these books. Anyway, it was interesting to know of one of the secret hiding compartments that my potential bride had, even if she had not told me about it herself.

As long as I didn't come across any really disturbing secrets in the house, the wedding was still on. Who am I kidding, she could have a fucking gingerbread house in the backyard and a talking black cat, and I would still be desperate to marry her. I added a few finishing touches to my proposal showroom, in the form of photographs I had taken of her. Capturing her beauty is an easy task, you just point and click, but these are my favourite ones of her, and I have quite a collection. Some people may have thought photos of the two of us would have been more fitting given the circumstances, but truth be told, we just did not have many pictures together. The piece de la resistance was scattered pink rose petals around the landing for where she walks in.

Chapter Seventeen

4 hours went by and it was safe to say my plan had hit a snag. She still was not home, she'd finished work 3 and half hours ago and I was just sat in her hallway watching the door. I did make myself useful, I unloaded and reloaded her dishwasher, did her ironing, arranged her DVDs

alphabetically and rearranged her bookcase by the colours on the spines. I tried to fix the jarred kitchen window but, made it worse. It is now slightly more open and inviting a persistent draft. Then it happened, keys rattled the lock on the door, significantly actually. She entered, my angel, she sways one way, then the other, bouncing from the wall to the staircase, zigzagging across the fake pink rose petals I had scattered along the floor. I don't think she noticed them.

She was clearly drunk. I was initially disappointed, I mean, is it even a truly consensual engagement if she said yes, would I have to do the whole thing again once she had sobered up? I asked myself knowing I would be asking her if she is sure several times a day regardless. A lot of the hard work decorating seemed to have gone unnoticed also, however, I had written 'LOVE' on her bathroom mirror and my lettering was shit. I had used her favourite lipstick to write with, so I tried to wipe it clear and just ended up smearing red all over the mirror, unfortunately it looked more threatening than romantic. I took a deep breath, it was time.

I stepped out of the doorway that I had been watching her from.

"Surprise!"

"Oh, my Jesus, FUCK, what the hell is wrong with you?"

"I...erm"

"Why are you in my house, why are you fucking lurking around the corner?

"I wasn't lurking, I was…"

"How did you get in here?"

"I broke in…through the kitchen window".

"Can you hear yourself?!"

"Look, I…"

"No, no, not look, just, what the fuck?!"

"If you'd just listen…"

"You broke into my house, what have you done to my mirror?"

"Yeah, I'm sorry about that, but hey, I emptied and filled your dishwasher".

"Dude! What the fuck? What is the matter with you?!"

"Please, this isn't…"

"You broke in to empty my dishwasher? And I'm not going to start on what you've done to my bookcase".

"Will you shut up?!"

I got down on one knee, and quickly pull out the ring "I know this may seem too soon, but I know you feel the same way as I do, so let's not waste any time...marry me?"

She looked around, she could have been in shock, maybe it was a moment of happiness, or it could have been sadness, perhaps it was that the room is spinning, and she needed to throw up. She slowly began nodding, as if she was rationalising what had happened, oh god. I thought to myself she's going to say yes, is she saying yes? I stood up, she remained looking down and then looked me in the eyes, she had a tear rolling down her cheek. The emotion of the situation had got to her, I grabbed her hand and slipped the ring on her engagement finger, she looked at it and began sobbing, which I think means she loved it. I took a deep breath and told her "I love you so much and I will never let you go".

Chapter Eighteen

The beach offered me little more than PTSD, the spot where Lainya had gone missing or at least where I last saw an item of hers had a torn down piece of police tape, half engulfed by sand between two metal rods which presumably the Melas police used to make a makeshift post. I hoped that this part of the investigation was over because it had quite clearly been a public walkway for quite some time considering the disturbances in the sand.

I felt hungry and purchased an ice cream cone and then instantly felt too anxious and worried to eat it, so I sat powerlessly by the harbour watching it melt. I am so tired, I really need some sleep, but I am worried I might miss an update, or unable to help Lainya should it become apparent she was in danger. It does not sit well with me, but I know I need to get some rest, so I am at the very least functional.

I walked back slowly to my room at the B&B. I was being sapped of energy by the sun, by stress, by the lack of food and sleep. I was trying to keep calm, but the rational part of my brain was telling me I am in real trouble. I felt like I was being watched with every step I took and while I knew I was being paranoid there was definitely an unusual amount of shady looking characters around, not that I could quantify what a usual number of shady characters should be. Maybe I am being watched. It would make sense at this stage of an investigation that I would still be the number one suspect in my wife's disappearance, she has made me watch enough murder documentaries to know that. Or maybe news is breaking around the island of who I am, 'there's the guy with the missing wife', the level of celebrity I have never wanted.

I got back to my room and just simply fell onto the mattress; I flopped and ignored my instincts to stop myself falling face first and shut my eyes. My whole body felt like it was tingling, presumably from exhaustion. I was sweating and desired the aircon be switched on, but I did not have the strength to move from the bed, so both will, and desire have been defeated by current ability. I just let myself go and really relaxed. The tingling in my body faded with my consciousness and the mattress became softer and embraced me.

I turned my head, and I could no longer hear the springs inside the mattress reacting as they cradled me, instead there was a smooth sound of tiny movements, like dainty muffled scratches. The more I focused and became aware of the sound the more the tingling sensation I had was replaced by ever so slight nipping. The smooth sound became an intense wriggling wave, squelching. I opened my eyes and my mattress had deformed itself into a hollow frame of maggots, eating the bedframe, biting at me, crawling into my ears, my nostrils, pouring into my screaming mouth and cartwheeling down my throat. I tried to hoist myself up but had no firm base to leverage myself up on, I was in a maggot pit, and they smothered me until all I could see is black.

Sweating profusely and breathing hard, I hit the floor with an uncomfortable slap, and instantly thrust around brushing myself down as if I was on fire. I hate anxiety nightmares. Despite myself I lifted the duvet of the bed just to reaffirm I was having a very nasty dream. I need a shower. I can still feel them crawling all over me. The problem with those kinds of nightmares is that because of how real they feel it makes you scared to lay down and close your eyes again, they leave you feeling vulnerable and shaken. Looking at the alarm clock on the bedside table I can see I was afforded a luxurious 10 minutes of sleep; guess I will have to chalk that off as a powernap and go and freshen up.

Having a shower did make me feel marginally better. whilst it obviously did not solve a single one of my problems, I at least felt awake and 'with it' again. I might even eat some fruit when I get back in the bedroom before going for another aimless crusade to find my wife. I filled my palm with a healthy serving of the accommodation's shampoo, body wash, bubble bath and lathered it through my hair before closing my eyes and going under the showerhead. This is the first time I have felt clean since I arrived on the island, especially considering 'sick gate' on the boat ride over here. That was probably a red flag that this holiday would be an unmitigated disaster.

As I stepped forward and turned the shower off, I just stood and closed my eyes and felt the last remaining drips of water cascade down my body. Being aware, present, and feeling sensations is good for my anxiety. I opened my eyes quickly as there were a few drops that sounded off, not loud, but I could tell they weren't water. They made a gentle thud sound rather than a dripping sound. I looked down to the shower basin and there were 4 little maggots floating to the plughole. I screamed and hopped out the shower and scrubbed myself with the towel to the point of nearly being red raw. Where the fuck did, they come from? What the hell?? They didn't come out of my hair surely?! I felt sick, I was instantly panicking again. I know I am not still sleeping, what the fuck? Okay, calm down, breathe, just think, and try to rationalise it.

I can't rationalise this, something awful is happening, or perhaps the maggots were a function of my slide into stress-induced insanity. I rushed back to plug hole and starred deep down into it as water was gargling down slowly and, sure enough, there were two maggots disappearing in the dark maze abyss of plumbing. The other two I either made up, or they went down the insect water slide first. So, I am not going crazy, but I am being tormented somehow.

Chapter Nineteen

My ordeal was not over, seeing those maggots in the plug hole and considering where they may have come from disgusted me. Following on from the anxiety dream I was in a very panicked state, my heart was racing, my breathing was heavy. I needed to be sick, and as the sink was closest, I rushed over and threw up what could have only been stomach lining mixed with coffee and a few licks of ice cream. Often when you have been sick you feel better for a while afterwards, however upon catching my pained reflection in the mirror I only felt worse, I stumbled back in shock and instant fear. The mirror had steamed over, which is to be expected, however, the word 'Lighthouse' has been written across the mirror. The word was not there seconds ago, while I was being sick.

Now I am really scared. I fixated on the water droplets running down from each letter, this means this was written recently, but this is a small bathroom, and I would notice if someone came in here and wrote on the mirror, they would have brushed past me in the doorway. This is not an old message revealed by the steam, this is new and recent, my eyes dart around the room looking for anything that could be an explanation, there is nothing. I scooped up my dry clothes that sat slumped on the toilet seat and walked hastily out the bathroom, incredibly freaked out.

The sight that greeted me in my main room only added to the escalating fright. My duvet had clearly been thrown across the room, my suitcase torn open, and all our belongings had been tossed around, although by the looks of it nothing had been taken. On the mattress were several copies of the same pamphlet from the tourist information stand, recommending a day trip to the lighthouse on the island. I sat on the foot of the bed in disbelief, clearly shaking, wishing I could run out of the room, but alas, I was naked and scared, frozen in fear. Just then, to further startle me, the TV turned itself on to a news report, I say startle, I let out a little scream when it suddenly lit up, I could not see the remote, I assumed I had sat on it, but it is nowhere to be seen.

The news story was just a repeat of a presenter saying, 'the lighthouse' then it would skip slightly, as if edited by ammeters, and say '11pm'. It would then continue to repeat that small clip over and over. I threw on my clothes, aware I was putting on the same underwear I was wearing before my shower, but not caring in the slightest. I had to get out of this room, and quick. I grabbed a pair of shorts and a t-shirt, launched them on too and bolted to the door. The TV was getting louder each time the man repeated the tiny segment, it was almost like he was screaming it at me as I got to the door. I was half expecting the door to be locked and for this horror to continue, but it opened, and I launched myself into the corridor. As the door slammed shut, I could no longer hear the TV, but the message rang clear in my ears. I ran outside of the B&B and did not stop running until I felt there was a safe distance between me and the building. I sat on a bench which presented me with a view of castle ruins being slowly taken back by Mother Nature maybe to be rediscovered hundreds of years from now. I was suddenly overcome with emotion, fear mainly, and sobbed into my hands, bewildered, and utterly lost. Alone.

I eventually gathered a level of composure, still shaken by the previous events, and desperate to tell someone, to try to rationalise what had happened, but also knowing they would think I am a lunatic, that I was somewhat detached from reality. Maybe I am, would I even know? I removed my face from my palms and slowly sat back, breathing in out and slowly, keeping my eyes closed. I let out one more long exhale and opened my eyes. I instantly nearly fell off the bench in shock as I realised a man was sat next to me.

"Jesus!"

"Not quite"

"Sorry, I didn't notice you..."

"Not at all, I am sorry. I did not mean to startle you".

"Yeah, well. Long day you know?"

"I am not hear to talk to you".

"Oh, right"

"We will talk, but now it is not safe for us to do so".

"Oh, for fucks sake what now? I've taken all..."

"Shut up! Sorry, please just be quiet. There is a pub called 'The Leaning Inn'. Meet me there tomorrow evening. I will be there from 8pm onwards. Please believe that I am a friend".

"Mate, at this stage I am pretty tired of questioning anything, I will be there".

"Never tire of questions, they are the only way one can seek the truth. However, there is a time and a place".

"Well, nothing is ever simple is it. See you tomorrow I guess".

"I know about your situation. Just know, you are not crazy".

I sat and watched him walk off. I can't believe I have made a friend without even trying. I really do not feel like having a pint, but I am definitely in the mood for some answers. The revelation that I was not crazy was as welcome as it perhaps should have been, it means something I do not understand is happening to me, and to my family. I glanced at my watch, still a few hours before the clock strikes 11, but despite reservations, I think I need to get to the lighthouse. Having time to spare was perfect, time for another cry. My rib cage feels like it is closing in on itself as if being crushed by a hand. I close my eyes and take deep breaths to try and stop the panic attack getting worse.

As night falls and darkness slowly dresses the land that was once full of colour and optimism provided by daylight, everything has now become rather sinister. I have never been 'scared' of the dark but I am definitely not fond of it, there is too much potential for jump scares, I guess. Think about it, that ally way you stroll down to work in the morning is non-threatening, almost jolly, depending on your attitude towards your employment. But walk back that way in winter months when it is dark and you can only just see the other side of it, well now it is a potential death trap, threats hidden by the cascade of darkness, shadows perfectly disguised by the pitch black, everything becomes a hiding place. The same principles can be applied in your own home, in the exposure of light, there is nothing to fear, nothing is hiding, but stay in that same position and there is a sudden power cut, and it feels like 'oh god, am I about to die?' Your home, your refuge, becomes a dark untrustworthy prison. The more I am thinking about this the more I realise, I fear the dark. Admitting it has not eased the burden, and walking towards the lighthouse presents the challenges expected by nightfall.

Chapter Twenty

The sound of the ocean is usually a welcome companion and offers tranquillity in a chaotic world, and while it eases the sense of loneliness for me personally, for others its vastness levels give a sense of insignificance. The ocean also offers a potential blanket of repetitive audio that could disguise sounds that my senses would normally react to. Simply put, in this current predicament it is not a welcome distraction, rather it adds to threat level which is very much maxed out. At least it is still mildly warm outside, I am still a bit frightened to return to my room back at the B&B. I really do not know what I am going to do about that, however, that is a future 'me' problem. Maybe I could ask to move rooms, politely request I am transferred to a room that is not haunted. Crazy as it sounds having a confirmed haunting would be a welcome justification, while ghosts are not something I have ever believed in I definitely would be happy to accept it as a rationale now to give me that peace of mind. I can say I have been victim to a haunting and turn off the fuzz in my brain that is still traumatised by what had happened, trying to figure itself out in the subconscious while I comprehend the current terror. When this is over, whatever this is that I am getting into I can reopen the haunting question and try and figure it out.

I was taken back slightly as some of the Melas wildlife ran across my path, I heard its paws pounding the floor only as it was within what I would class as striking distance. I am not sure it even noticed me as it galloped past me and towards the decline of the hillside. I was in awe of how big it was, it was running on all fours, but I would say if it was stood on its hindlegs it would easily stand at 5ft tall. I have never seen a creature like it, essentially it looked like a huge sphynx cat, but it had a tail that looked like an arrow, and its facial features were almost human. I pondered the identity of this magnificent beast. While it is quite a startling sight in nightfall, my love of animals made the chance encounter a welcomed addition to my journey.

From a distance the lighthouse gives off an enticing glow, hopefully the boats do not find it enticing, but it looks as if the ground around it is safe and protected by its glow. The closer I get the more the glowing ground fades and is replaced with obscurity. While I am under tremendous psychological strain, I can't ignore how regal the lighthouse looks. Although I am utterly dwarfed by the infrastructure and that just adds to the vulnerability I am feeling. I don't know what I am supposed to do now that I am here. Perhaps I should have picked up one of the many brochures that the poltergeist spread over my maggot pit mattress. I walked up to the door and instantly recognised the symbol etched into the wood. I don't know what it means, but I recognise it from the function room where I spoke to police. Okay, the plan is to keep going and do whatever it takes to find my wife, reunite her with our daughter and then confess everything that has happened. At that stage I will be locked up on a psychiatric ward and get the help I so clearly need, but at least my wife and baby will be together and safe.

The lighthouse door is locked. I walk around the circumference, and I expertly dodge some nettles at the last second but trip slightly on uneven ground. If someone is here to attack me, I am certainly putting on a show for them. I really do not know what to do. I hold my hands out by my side, and limply say "hello?" It comes out quite quiet and rather squeaky, I try again, a bit more assertive "hello?" Same outcome, radio silence. I stroll slowly to the cliff side; I had a perverse interest in how high it was and how much danger I would be in if I fell. All I could see was black which tells me I am high up here, and, stating the obvious, it is nighttime. I throw down a rock and wait to hear it hit ground or splash, I hear neither. But I was never going to hear anything over the sound of the waves. And it is reasons like that, amongst many, many others, why I would not survive in the wild.

I turned back towards the lighthouse, and was stunned, my breath withdrew so much that I felt like I had been winded, before me was a lady with her back turned to me. Long blonde hair, bare foot, she did not need to turn around, I knew instantly it was Lainya. I have found her! Thank God, I have found her. I couldn't speak because I was so chocked up and happy, tears streamed down my cheeks, racing one and other to my jawbone before leaping off. All the emotion of the last few days was concluding. I took some steps forward ready to embrace her and never let go. She slowly turned around. Something was wrong. "Lainya?" She didn't speak, something was off about her, "Honey?" Her eyes, they just looked right through me as if I wasn't there "hey, sweetheart it's me!" She smiled a little, thank God, it has registered. Still, something seemed wrong, her smile was not a happy one, it was almost a smirk, conniving. Then she broke out into a sprint.

I opened my arms to hug her, to grab her and squeeze her, but she ran straight past me, "Lainya?!" I glanced back, was she being chased? No one was there, I turned back to Lainya, she was still sprinting, towards the edge of the cliff, "Lainya, no, what the fuck, Lainya it's a cliff, stop! FUCKING STOP" I broke out in a sprint, I had to catch her "Lainya stop!!! Please don't, don't do this please". She leapt forward just as I dived to try and grab her ankle missing by centimetres, pearling dangerously over the cliff top, Lainya went into a swan dive motion, it all went by so slowly, she looked angelic. Then she fell into the blackness "Lainya no!! Fuck, FUCK NO, FUCKING NO" I screamed until my throat went horse, I screamed so hard that my body rejected my instincts to continue screaming and went into a coughing fit finished only by vomiting. I laid hugging the corner of the grass verge, crying so hard my whole body was shaking with each tear. I just kept repeating "Lainya no, why god why" over and over again.

I got to my feet, trying to keep my eyes open, for every second they closed I could just see her falling again and again. I looked up to the lighthouse and was further taken back as there were two figures stood by the glass ceiling looking down on me. I recognised them instantly. It was the fisherman who booked me into the B&B, so he isn't dead, and by his side was a cloaked figure which may or may not have been my dressing gown, what is going on? Is everyone on this island mentally torturing me?! Well, this is enough, despair has turned to rage, if you want me fuckers, you got me!

I ran to the lighthouse door and threw my shoulder into it, the door opened with an ease that suggested it had been opened since I had previously rattled the handle. I would have normally baulked at the amount of the steps, but my adrenaline was pumping, and I glided up them, 3 steps at a time, like a helter-skelter in reverse. I got to the ladder and threw myself to the latch to get into the lantern room. It was heavier than expected but I was in no mood for being blocked and managed to force my way in. I must have bumped my head about 8 times, but I did not care, nor did I acknowledge the pain long enough for it to last. I got in the room, but they were not there, I ran around the cylindrical room, casting a frantic shadow against the optic device. They are not here how is this even possible?! It's a lighthouse, there is only one entrance, and it happens to also be the only exit. They would have had to pass me on the stairs. I know I am not seeing things. I can't take much more of this, where are they? And Lainya, my sweet, beautiful Lainya. I start screaming "Where are you, show yourselves! You wanted my attention well you got it, where are you?" I am irrationally lashing out now, kicking the beacon and screaming. I heard voices from the entrance to the lighthouse, I was not aware it was the police until they reached me, I ran over and grabbed one of them, "help me, please help me, my wife, she was here, she leapt of the cliff and then there was this fisherman, and oh god, just please…", he effortlessly pushed me off him, gave me a sympathetic look and punched me square in the jaw.

Chapter Twenty-one

I awoke confused and groggy, my head throbbing, I had been sweating profusely, and my jaw is aching from where I was punched by that policeman when I…oh god, "Lainya" I shot up in my bed as the unbearable memory came flooding back. I am back in my room. How did I get back here. I have taken more than I could endure. I slumped back down onto my mattress, murmuring my wife's name, I could not care less about the fisherman and his random disappearance anymore, how am I going to tell my daughter that mummy is gone? I still do not understand it myself.

Just then the toilet flushed, I am not alone in my room, "hello??", the taps are running, "Erm, hello??" The bathroom door handle begins to turn, then the door opens a creak. I take a deep breath, given the events since I arrived here, I need to be prepared for anything although there is no fight left in me. Out walked the policeman who had knocked me out, drying his hands on one of my t-shirts I had left on the bathroom radiator to dry.

"Ah good, you're awake, sorry about the old knockout blow back in the lighthouse, you were getting a little hysterical you know. Didn't want to draw any further attention to the situation or things coulda...well, things can have a habit of escalating. You have been asleep for about 9 hours, I said I would stay here until you woke up. So if you are okay I will get off now, oh and here's some change, I ate your chocolate bar, sorry to literally eat, shit and leave"

"Hold on!"

"Is that not enough money to cover it?"

"I don't care about the fucking chocolate bar! My wife committed suicide in front of my eyes! I don't feel like we can ignore that".

"Look, the best thing to do is..."

"Look nothing! I need your help".

"I really wanted to avoid this, listen I am going to say this and then I will have to be asked to be removed from this case and not see you again. Your wife isn't dead, and also, I am sorry".

For the second time in 9 hours, I am powerless as his fist hurtles towards my jaw.

Before last night I had never been punched in the face, however, I am now waking up after being knocked out for a second time by the same guy. Feeling woozy and pissed off I crawl across the floor and rummage through my suitcase for some pain killers. The headache and jaw ache are unreal and it is safe to say it has not improved my mood. So, the police on this island have a frustrating way of handling investigations. But apparently Lainya is not dead, and even though the words came from a man who was very keen to throw fists, I believed him. I just feel that I would know if she was no longer with us. I would know. But who was that person who dived off the cliff and why did she look exactly like my wife?

I think being knocked out twice has done me a favour, aside from the headache I feel pretty well rested for the first time since Lainya went missing. Once the pain killers kick in, I am going to just aimlessly walked around the island. See if I notice anything that could help me locate Lainya, I can't just sit here doing nothing while she is missing. I went to the bathroom, and the colour of my urine told me I could do with getting a glass of water. I checked my reflection and noticed I had some slight bruising but nothing too harsh on my cheek. Nothing to suggest I had been in a fight. Well, fight is generous, nothing to suggest I had been knocked out twice is more accurate.

Feeling refreshed for the first time since arriving here I further indulged in self-care and brushed my teeth. I do not know why but I always wander around while brushing my teeth. It is not that I am searching for an epiphany or a special lightbulb moment, I just don't feel comfortable standing in the mirror watching myself brush my teeth. Having successfully covered all my room and reached an uncomfortable level of foam in my mouth I returned to the sink. I spat out the toothpaste but instantly recoiled as the plug to the bathroom sink was full of maggots. They seemed to be heaving and convulsing as if the plug hole was about to explode and fire thousands of them towards the ceiling. Then the mirror caught my eye, the words 'next time, you fall' had been written. The difference this time was it wasn't steamy in the bathroom. This had been smeared on the mirror in what looked like blood and I'm telling myself it is tomato sauce although my instincts beg to differ, it is blood.

Naturally I panic. And now I feel like I am being targeted by, well, God knows what?! Are ghosts real? There is no way anyone got in the bathroom while I was brushing my teeth. Maybe it's a hoax?? That must be it. Pretty sick game to play on a man who is searching for his missing wife. If I end up on some kind of prank show on TV I am suing for unfathomable psychological distress.

Fear is a strange thing, I am absolutely terrified right now, but I am not as scared as last time this happened. I guess some things are always scary but if you are subjected to them enough the fear subsides slightly. Walking back into the room I stand corrected and am scared out of my mind again. The room has been completely trashed but not by t-shirts being thrown and pamphlets, it looks like a wild animal has been in here. The mattress is torn down the middle, a bunch of my t-shirts are ripped to shreds, the curtains are torn, my suitcase has gashes across it. The double mirror sliding wardrobe doors opposite my bed have large red letters smeared across them 'next time, you die!!!' as if there was any doubt to what the message in the bathroom mirror meant. I hope the B&B don't charge me for this. But then how do I explain? This time I don't grab clothes and run. I have either given up, or I am now pissed off enough to fight.

I pace back and forth like an agitated caged animal in a zoo, just recapping everything in my mind, hoping some of it will make sense. I have come on holiday with my wife and little girl. My wife has gone missing, the police say I shouldn't question it and see what happens, and I am now getting death threats from an unknown entity that can write messages and destroy a room in seconds, without making a sound. I wonder who will play me in the film adaptation of my life? I am half scared to my wits end and half, almost, amused by how ridiculous this is. It is not long now until I need to go to the pub and meet the stranger from the bench who alluded to knowing something about Lainya.

I do not know what to do about my room as it is a hard one to flag to the reception and while it would be ideal to change rooms there is a bit too much going on here to try to explain. And it would definitely be too much to explain and expect any understanding. I am still flirting with the idea that I am on the steady decline to madness, and sadly that is the most rational explanation. If that is not the case, then I can safely say I have been through, and seen some shit.

I look around the room and the majority of my smarter clothes seem to have been torn by the fashion-conscious poltergeist that took issue with a short sleeve pink linen shirt. I have no real desire to smarten up anyway, I will just head out in what I am wearing. Despite anxiety levels being through the roof and against my better judgement, I am having a cup of coffee. I would love to be able to close my eyes, sip some water, and listen to the distant ocean waves rolling back and forth, but anytime I close my eyes too long I can still see Lainya or at least the fake Lainya, Fainya? jumping off the cliff side. The fact is, even though I know in my heart that was not my wife, I still witnessed a person hurtle themselves to their death, and that is pretty traumatising. Mix that with everything else that is going on and it is no wonder I might be going a bit bonkers.

The heat in the room is reaching an uncomfortable level of warmth, almost like I have a fever, instinctively I know something is trying to spook me further and I am just bemused. I watch the paint on the ceiling begin to bubble as the heat in the room continues to rise. The lights in the room begin to violently click on and off, prompting me to leave. I find myself staring into the corner of the room where the light bulb in the lamp had just exploded. My train of thought is broken by the thrashing sound of both taps in the bathroom suddenly turning on and spanking the sink basin. Spray from the intensity covers the wall and the occasional drip has a maggot wriggling alongside it. God, I hate maggots. I walk into the bathroom and turn the taps off, and purposefully don't look in the mirror. "Jokes on you, I was going out anyway" I say out loud to absolutely no one. My brief moment of cockiness is cancelled out by the scurried haste in which I leave the room.

Chapter Twenty-Two

Lainya is always the strongest one out of the two of us, she always took the lead, she was assured and confidant and just strode ahead. I was the lovesick puppy, trying to keep up, dancing around her shadow and just happy to be existing in her space. I did not like making decisions, talking on the phone, or generally anything that would have been useful. Maybe she wasn't strong, maybe she had to be strong. I feel so bad, so guilty, that I got her for a wife, and all she got in return was me.

A year before our daughter was born her father died and she was devastated, naturally. I was impartial about it, I would not have wished it on him of course, mainly because of how much she loved him, but I certainly do not miss being threatened by him constantly, calling me a creep, telling me to stop hanging around his daughter. He probably thought he was doing her a favour, but what was actually going on was that he was a prick. Her mother is wonderful though, mums generally are.

My wife comes from a very big family the majority of whom do not seem to like me. A lot of the husbands that have married into this family are rich, decisive and take the lead. they look down on men like me, a follower. They are all successful go getters who challenge everything life has to throw at them. I am the person who is sometimes too anxious to leave the house and just forcing myself to do so takes the same level of strength they display; it is just not recognised. on the day of her father's funeral and because of my status in this family, I did not travel in the very compact family car that follows the hearse, and I made my own way there. To this day I do not know if that was a mistake. I assumed she would be supported by all her family and I think she was, they were all sharing the same grief. Ultimately, I was not supporting her, but at the time I thought I was being helpful by stepping back. Not being in the way. But it would not be the first time my judgement has been clouded by my poor mental health.

Everybody entered the church and sat down, I was surprised at how many people had turned up, was he popular and just hated me, or was he a total arsehole and 90% of the attendees here just want to enjoy talking about him being dead?

Lainya was at the front with her mother, three sisters and big brother. I did not manage to make it to a pew, as it was so busy, so I stood at the back and respectfully kept my head down, staying quiet, and agonising over the fact that I could not remember if I had turned off the tumble dryer at home. Best case scenario would be that my electric bill was higher that month, worst case scenario my house burns to the ground and my joined neighbour's house too, killing all inside. That would have suck. I wish I could have thought about anything else then, I wish I wasn't the way I am, there was the service going on and my instincts were telling me to run and check the electric was off. I felt sick.

Towards the end of the service, I looked forward towards Lainya. I could see she was looking around, her eyes locked onto mine and her face dropped. She almost seemed shocked to see me, her lip quivered like I was a ghost, she knew I would be here, as if I would leave her alone on this day. She seemed to shake her head slightly before she began to cry. A daughter crying at their father's funeral is not that strange, but for some reason I feel like it was me being there, unannounced at the back that upset her. That is the only time I have ever seen her vulnerable, and I hated it.

As soon as the curtain went around the coffin, I quietly made my exit at the back taking great care to not interrupt anybody paying their respects. I was unable to stand seeing her so upset. And the way she looked at me as if I was the cause of the pain, I do not think I could handle that again. I reminded myself that grief is a complex beast, and she will have a lot of emotions to contend with, that her reaction was most likely nothing to do with me at all. I made a promise to myself that day to do better, always do better.

The only good news was that I had remembered to turn off the tumble dryer.

Chapter Twenty-Three

The pub where I was meeting my mysterious friend was in fitting with the rest of the architecture in Melas. The beauty was appreciated despite me being on a mission for answers. The structure was crooked, weathered with age, and battered by the elements. Lainya would love the look of this place, when I find her, and if she is okay, I am going to bring her here for our first celebratory drink. It was the Tudor design again, leaning slightly to the right, with its upper floor leaning slightly forward as if it is ingesting its clientele. The upper floor is littered with tiny little windows which have been blacked out, but the intricate details are there, like a fly's eyes. I took a deep breath and entered 'The Leaning Inn'.

The inside had not had a modern refurbishment which I was happy about. There was a fantastic fireplace to my right which I can imagine in winter has a roaring fire, the belly of the beast inviting you in with its four dusty reading chairs and accompanying side tables to bestow your drink upon. Etched in the wooden pillars of the fireplace is a testament to the island heritage, fisherman holding aloft...a trout? A sea bass? I don't know anything about fishing, a fisherman holding up his catch of the day. And on the other side a ship sailing over waves with a slight spray coming from the underbelly of the boat as it protested to the oceans current. Across the mantel piece was, of course, a ship in a bottle. Obviously, it was old, or perhaps it is more polite to say it was vintage, an antique. The sails on the little model were torn and yellowing, the ship had signs of breakage and was slightly dismounted from its stand. Above the fireplace was a large mirror and, matching the ambience of the pub, it looked as if it had been forgotten by time, the craftsmanship of the frame matched by the layers of dust it had gathered. It looked as if it was growing cardboard, it was that thick. As my eyes began to wander away from the fireplace I noticed, again, etched into the wood that symbol I have seen so many times on this island. The same one I noticed in the function room, the same as at the lighthouse, here again. I wonder what its history is.

I walked up to the bar. The barman turned around and looked me up and down. He slammed both his fists down onto the bar and stood leaning into it, and he continued to stare at me as if waiting for me to initiate conversation. I opened my mouth to speak when he suddenly smiled and spoke "hello my friend, what can I get you?" His voice was husky and reeked of cigar smoke, I bet he drinks whisky as if it's water. "Could I just have an orange juice please, no ice?" he stared back at me, at this moment I did not know if he was about to burst out laughing or slit my throat. He coughed a little gentle rhythm to clear his throat "my friend we don't serve juice, we are not a pub for children"

"Are there any pubs for children?"

"my friend! What REAL drink can I get for you?". I sensed he wasn't a fan of my dry witted sarcasm.
"Okay, please could I have a vodka with lemonade?"
Again, he slammed his hands down on the table.

"You have a pure soul and a good spirit, now I would never water that down, a good spirit is one to be embraced and celebrated. Now, I am the barman, I have many spirits, good spirits, ones that should not be watered down! Now I will ask a final time, my very good friend what can I get you to drink?". Everyone on this fucking island is nuts. Jesus this is intense. I am not really a spirit drinker. I fear if I mention that I will hastily be toppled out of the Leaning Inn.

I stood scanning the bar, I had met the uncomfortable and unnecessary last chance saloon before, well I do not know, at the very least I will be asked to leave by a very pissed off barman. Suddenly, a saviour, who just so happened to be my new pal whom I was here to meet. He stood beside me, slammed down his pint pot and said, "same again Lucas, and one for him as well." He nodded in my direction and then patted me on the shoulder. At this stage I wished two things, I wish his sudden appearance and slamming of pint pot hadn't so obviously startled me, and I wish I didn't have the urge to bury my head in his chest and weep. Bar man Lucas pulled us two very thick, sludgy, tar like pints and smiled at us both while watching them settle before topping them up, the thickness of the stout emphasised by how hard he was pulling the tap. Although he seemed passionate about his vocation, maybe being eccentric was part of his act. I smiled as I lifted my pint, and he swiftly grabbed my forearm causing me to spill a little of my drink. We locked eyes and he said, "just because something does not seem worth exploring that is not to say you won't find heart in the experience". This was oddly profound and incredibly over the top in regard to a beer. The parting comment did make me wonder if he was aware of my current predicament.

I followed the friendly stranger across to a table which I had not noticed him sat at previously, although I was somewhat preoccupied by the fireplace, so I am not going to put that down as another strange occurrence of this island. I had a mouthful of the drink, and it was dreadful. I now had to commit to a pint of this sludge just to be polite. He looked at me, a coy grin on his face "you like?" "What is this?" "It's special to our island, a stout made with oysters, squid ink" he then slapped his palm on the table and shouted, "with bull testicals!" before flexing his, admittedly, impressive bicep. I let out a fake laugh as some sort of acknowledgment to his bravado and to the realisation I had to drink this.

"Look, I'm going to cut to the chase here, are you the one who left me that message in the mirror while I showered?"

"Excuse me?!?" His face turned into a combination of shock, anger, and bewilderment.

"Oh, never mind" clearly not him, don't know what I was thinking. I'll blame the testosterone from my bull testical ocean stout. Right, regroup and try again. I need answers.

"Your wife is not dead; she is however missing." I was about to snap at him for stating the obvious, but I needed to manage my emotions, this is obviously an important discussion, and I may need this guy, I had to be mature and manage this relationship. I cleared my throat, half to prevent a prepubescent squeak escaping my oesophagus which always coincides with adrenaline pumping through my system, and half to compose myself and control my breathing. I looked him right in the eyes and said sternly "where is she?" On appearance alone he would destroy me in a physical altercation, but I think I would be able to summon some form of desperate superior combat skill given the emotional state I am in. "That, I do not know" he responded to my asking.

"If I knew where you wife was, we would be there now, not here, drinking. It's important you know this island has a very long history. A beautiful history, but equally a troubled history, a very, very troubled history. Things sometimes happen here that simply cannot be explained, some call them mysteries, other refer to old fables and legends when we celebrate our beginnings. But make no mistake, life works differently in Melas, and...and...I am really worried for you and your family. People have gone missing here before, tourists have gone missing here before, but..." then he leaned in towards me to whisper, spitting slightly on my lip as he continued "the authorities have a good way of making questions and suspicions go away, some call it a cover up for the protection of the island, others say it's corruption, a corruption so deeply rooted that even the most senior members of authority are in on it. Now the problem here, and the reason I am so worried for you is because you have asked questions, the people of the island are aware of your presence here. The more you wonder the deeper in trouble I feel you will be".

"So, let me get this straight, what you're telling me is I shouldn't be searching for my wife? My wife who is missing? I shouldn't ask questions and just shrug my shoulders? Go home and put it down as a bad holiday experience but leave a good review so I don't piss off the fucking island?! Is that what you're telling me?"

"I understand your anger and your frustration, but I implore that your keep your voice down. I beg that of you. I want to help. Count to 10 and casually look around the room".

I found myself following his command. I wanted to know where he was going with this bullshit. I noticed a man at the bar sat on a stool who was looking at me and then swiftly looked away. Another man who was sat by the piano nursing an empty pint glass swiftly turned away once I looked at him and lifted the glass to create the illusion that he was drinking. Finally, a couple of gents playing chess suddenly engaged in their game when I glanced in their direction although neither of them had made a move. I turned back to my friend, rolling my head and pushing my arms out to give the impression that my actions had been a random stretch.

"You are being watched. As I say, you have been loud and desperate, and you have made your presence known. Now, I truly believe your wife is alive, and I am hoping you can keep a low profile and maybe one day you and your wife can take your pram home and put this dreadful experience behind you".

"This is fucking insane; we've come here for a holiday! We went through a fucking travel agent and now you're telling me I've caused a ruckus by searching for my missing wife, like that's unusual?! Or that it's caused offence to the people who live on the island where tourists apparently go missing. News flash mate, people don't go missing! So, what happens to them?!"

He looked down at his pint, took a deep breath and suddenly all the prowess of this man bear with huge biceps swept away, his shoulders sunk, and he looked like a frightened schoolboy awaiting the cane from a Victorian headmaster. He was whispering to himself and shaking his head slowly then he suddenly stamped his foot and looked me directly in the eyes, his eyes bloodshot red, wide, and full of tears and he said to me in a chocked voice "sacrifice".

"Sacri- wait? What?! No. We need to go to the police. You! Need to tell the police". He reached across the table and slapped me "you haven't listened, the police are involved, stop making noise, stop being a problem, for yours and your wife's sake shut the fuck up!" I should have been given that advice on my wedding day. "I didn't know there would be these people here watching, this place is usually a safe venue to gather, I wish I could tell you more, one day I will, tell me, aside from your wife going missing has anything unusual happened while you have been here?" I had to think, where to start? and the further I went down this path the more freaked out I was becoming and I needed to get out, I was having a panic attack. I stood up "I need to get some fresh air." I was grabbed on the forearm, his mighty fist easily wrapping around my wrist "I would not do that right now, please, just stay safe and take your time" I understood and sat there head in hands breathing slow, using the techniques I know that work. "When we arrived, I checked into the B&B and it was very old fashioned looking, the next day when I went in, it was brand new. I was checked in by an old fisherman whom I was later told had died a very long time ago. There was a cloaked figure which I rationalised was my dressing gown on my baby cam, there was a message written on my bathroom mirror and then there's this whole lighthouse thing which I am still too traumatised to detail. Oh my god, this island actually is fucked. Are ghosts real?! Why is this happening?"

"As I keep saying, you've made yourself known to this island and the wheels are in motion"

"What the fuck is that supposed to mean? Where is my wife?!?"

"Please, please, please, stay calm. I know this is a lot". When he said these words I noticed a tattoo on his wrist, in fact not a tattoo, a scar, it looked like a burn, but I recognised the symbol straight away. "And what the fuck is the symbol I keep seeing everywhere?" He stopped dead in his tracks and looks astonished, his lower lip began to quiver as his hastily pulled his sleeve over his wrist again "you've seen this symbol before?" "Yes, I see the fucking thing everywhere. What does it mean?" He sat back down and began sobbing uncontrollably. I sat, rather uncomfortably. I did not know if I should rub his arm to console him or tell him to shut up and tell me what it means. "If you can see the symbol, it is already too late for you

Chapter Twenty-Four

I have been outside of the pub for about 15 minutes now. I still can't wrap my head around what had been said or what had happened. After telling me it was essentially 'too late to save me' I ended up sat opposite this crying mountain of man, rubbing his arm, and telling him I will be fine, and everything is okay. He recoiled at my touch and apologised several times before standing up, almost in a trance like state, it was like he had lost all sense of where he was and what he had just been telling me. I then sat and watched, flabbergasted as he walked out the pub and I became genuinely scared for my life. I felt like I wasn't safe anywhere, certainly not on this island. But I don't own a boat, and I damn sure am not leaving here without Lainya and the baby, so for now, I am stuck here. My inadequate survival mode needs to kick in. I stood up and the other gentleman in the pub were now being more blatant about watching me and, naturally, I was made to feel extremely uncomfortable by this.

I walked out of the pub and instantly started into a sprint, aimlessly running as fast as I could to put as much distance between me and the pub as quick as possible. I slowed down, mainly because my fitness levels and recent diet of fasting through sadness did not lend itself to maintaining a sprint. I looked back and I could see all the men from the pub, stood side by side smiling and waving at me. This really scared me. The smile was not a fond smile, it was more of an unnerving smirk of a group of people that knew something I didn't. The waving was perfectly synchronised as if to say run but you can't hide. I have no idea what is going on, but I sense this island is going to chew me up and spit me out. I don't know what I have done to deserve this, maybe I insulted its history by throwing up the entire way here, but that was merely a reflection of my travel sickness, not an act intended to insult the place. It certainly does not warrant my family and I being offered up for sacrifice and torment. If that is their intention towards us. Whoever they may be.

I felt threatened, like I was in real danger. It felt like everyone had stopped in their tracks and were just stood staring at me. Not stopping to think, I carried on running through instinct, with mine telling me that I would be hurt standing still. My lack of athleticism means this is a short-term plan at best. My adrenaline carries me further than I thought was possible but is still significantly less than how far I could have gone in my twenties.

I had hoped my aimless sprinting would eventually lead to the ocean and considering I am on an island the odds were in my favour, hopefully then I may have some serenity. Alas, the continued fuckery of my holiday meant it wasn't to be. I instead ended up by a mouldy fence which was encapsulating a thick and daunting woodland area. Woods in the evening are never a good shout, even when things are going well in life, so I continued to survey my surroundings while hunched over breathing heavy and leaning on my knees which hummed ever so slightly to the tune of my muscle spasms. The fence was the only feature I could identify as the land before me continued to stretch. It was odd how the grass on the other side of the fence seemed to yellow slightly, as if it was dying. Maybe this particular bit of land didn't belong to the island, so the natives neglect it.

I jumped back as there was sudden movement near my feet, and while I think it is forgivable for me to be so jumpy currently, I didn't need to be, it was just a cat, a black cat at that, so with the looming darkness of night it was able to approach me undetected. "I do not have any food kitty and I am shitty company". I would normally applaud myself for that dope rhyme and then spend a good 10 minutes in my head thinking of words that rhyme with company to keep it going, suffice to say, I am not in the mood right now. The cat began making an eerie meowing noise while its stomach heaved in and out and its neck pulsated. Now, I have never owned a cat, so I have no idea why this happening "oh for goodness' sake, please don't fucking die. Don't tell me you came all this way over to me to just die" it had not, it was throwing up at my feet, the smell was horrific, "what have you been eating?" looking down at my feet

I notice the majority of the vomit was moving, as it is made up of maggots. I looked over at the cat that was now walking towards the woods, it paused to look at me, silently imploring me to follow it, I shook off the maggots from my trainers and started towards the cat, "alright you little bastard, message received, I'm coming." I follow the cat, for reasons I don't fully understand, but it seems to make sense. If I die in these woods, at least I finish the holiday the way I started it, with vomit on trainers.

Chapter Twenty-Five

The woods were an ominous presence, the trees were thick and stocky and the top of them intertwined together like knitwear. I imagine that even in daylight it would be pretty dark in here because of the natural ceiling created by the knotted branches. I continuously lose my footing as the surface is a perfect patchwork of ivy, moss, rotting tree stumps, mushrooms, and overgrown shrubs. I can easily picture that this is what the world looked like before the infestation of humanity ruined it beyond repair. The protective roof of branches has caused it to be really cold in here but that has not prevented the atmosphere being rather humid and subsequently all the live vegetation has an almost sweaty texture to it causing my feet to slip beneath as I endeavour forwards.

I am using my mobile phone torch to try and follow this feline that I sense is some sort of messenger. I am aware at how crazy that notion is, but having been terrified for so long I am questioning less and accepting whatever happens next. I haven't had any signal for days, but I still carried my phone in my pocket. I lie to myself saying it is in case I suddenly get signal. I further lie to myself saying having it in my pocket is a habit. The truth is my phone is an addiction. And being 'off the grid' while all this has been happening has further induced my anxiety levels. I have had no route to escapism that a quick scroll on the internet could have provided, I have found information harder to come by, and research has been impossible. But ultimately, not having my phone in my pocket would have felt weird.

In the 10 minutes that have passed I have fallen over more times than I can count. I am uneasy on my feet like a toddler learning to walk. I have scratches and a gash down both forearms, my hands are sore and muddy, and I have had so many branches slap me across the face I swear I could hear the trees laughing. The foundations are becoming thicker with sloppy mud and oversized plant life, and the moss I have repeatedly fallen into seems to have stained my skin and, causing it to itch incessantly. This is up there with the worst parts of the worst holiday, possibly of all time actually. I do not know what determines if an area is a wood or a forest, but whichever is worse in terms of being an accommodating habitat this is that.

One thing I do notice is that I have been following this cat for some time and there is still no sign of a footpath or an obvious area where the woodland shrubs have been trampled enough to look like it is a walkway. Nobody is passing through here, admittedly I am quite deep in and the torch on my phone only provides enough light for my next step, but I am fed up with tripping up and stumbling into trees. Roots seems to be moving to trip me up at will. I know I am now at the height of my paranoia. I have an inner conflict of how much I can trust my own eyes and senses. I ache, I am tired, I am bleeding, but like an intoxicated person determined to get home I just focus all my energy into taking the next step, nothing more, nothing less. I used to dream of seeing an area of earth like this, that seems to have been devoid of human contamination for decades. Now I am here I can ascertain that it is an underwhelming experience to say the least.

The cat begins its nausea dance once more which gives me the opportunity to have a quick breather. It leaves a fresh pile of maggots on the floor, which is so gross, however I am becoming slightly desensitised to the sight of maggots now. Yes, they are disgusting but more than anything I am just sick of the sight of them. The cat then shoots up a tree, displaying such ease and grace it is almost like it is flying up there, galloping against the bark. And then I can no longer see it. The light my phone emits is nowhere near powerful enough to see up a tree especially considering how far from any obviously entrance I am. "Kitty? kitty come back." I have only ever had dogs before, so I made a gentle whistling sound to encourage it back to me and continue its role of tour guide, once it did not reappear, I tried sucking my lips together to make an enticing friendly pet owner kind of noise, but all this did was look like I was puckering up. If I was the cat at this stage, I would have taken what remained of my 9 lives and ran away as quick as possible. I can safely assume the cat is not going to come back, and that is if it is even still up there. So that has happened, I am all alone, abandoned in the dark by a cat. I know contextually it is a strange time to develop abandonment issues, but here we are.

I spin around quickly with my phone held aloft as I hear someone, or something clear its throat. And there he is, stood about 50 metres from me, the fisherman, the same one who booked me into my B&B, the same one from the lighthouse, who also happens to appear on a 200-year-old photograph. The ghoul of Melas "Hello, so it appears ghosts are real? What do you want with me motherfucker?" I say, surprisingly pulling off the interrogation without my voice squeaking, although it was a strange thing to call an entity. He says nothing, he never does. He turns and walks away. I stumble after him, the sense of danger builds with each step, but I feel I have no other options than to follow.

I take about 15 steps forwards, and I am suddenly blocked by a falling body that stops with an uncomfortable snapping sound and seemingly floats rigidly before me. Wait, not floating, hanging, oh shit. I look up, it is my friend from the pub. What the hell? "Fuck, shit, shit! hold on, I will get you down, don't panic" I know he is already dead, I just had to say something. I frantically try to find some part of the tree I could use for leverage to get him down. The ground is now perfectly flat and there nothing I can do. I try to get a foot up on the thick roots of the tree, but it is too slippery, excessively so. "I am so sorry; I am so fucking sorry you felt you had to do this. We spent the night talking about me, we could have talked about you as well, what was going on in your life that made this seem the only way out. Maybe things would have been different if we had talked longer" I looked him in the face properly and recoiled as I realised both his eyes had been gouged out. I instantly span around to throw up. I looked over again and his jaw dropped open. His detached eyeballs rolled out of his mouth and hit the ground and began to bubble up and melt into the soil. His tongue had been removed, and his forearm that contained the symbol on it had been sliced open and thick chunks of skin had been removed so that the symbol was no longer a part of his body. "Jesus" this wasn't a suicide, this was murder, "who did this to you?" I have seen too much; this is too much horror to withstand. I drop to the floor and sob just inches below his dangling feet.

Chapter Twenty-Six

I somehow gather some form of composure and decide I have to keep moving even though my body has become incredibly heavy and warning me to stay still, I am a father I can't give up. I gently pass the hanging body towards where the fisherman was waiting for me, "I am so sorry" I say as I brush past his body causing it to twirl slightly. He did not deserve for this to be his fate. The fisherman stands up ahead with his back to me, waiting but not willing to engage with the trauma around him. As I continue walking towards the fisherman, I hear the hanging man's voice gurgling out "it is already too late for you", repeating his last words to me at the pub. I tell myself it is just my mind playing tricks on me, but deep down, in line with everything else that has happened, I know somehow, he is actually saying it. An impressive feat considering he is dead and missing his tongue. Dark humour is now keeping me sane, disguising the fact I am more frightened than I have ever been and that things are happening now that are very, very real. The disrespect however makes me worry about the karma if it is real. I continue forward, bloodied, bruised, bleeding and shaking.

We got to what seemed like a cross junction within the woodland. There was a glow to right which lit up the surroundings a little, I was astonished to see an idyllic little cottage sat there, cuddled by bushes. Its straw roof interrupted by a stone chimney which was smoking enough to suggest someone was home. What the hell. Who would live here?! Why has that even been built here? So many questions, no one to answer them, plus I haven't got the energy to engage even if I did have someone here to answer them. It is easier on my mind to just start accepting things now, any kind of resistance is gone as I am not strong enough.

I look over to the fisherman and he is staring at me, but through me, soulless, he is pointing upwards. He was pointing at the branches of the trees that form this cross section which have combed together and combined to make a rugged depiction of the symbol I have been seeing everywhere. The dreaded symbol. I look back to the fisherman "right, very good. What do you want me to say?". He does not respond, I did not really expect him to, but I did wonder if I tried to casually engage with him if he might offer something, anything. He then points to the cottage, I guess that is where all this has been heading. "Well, I guess we go our separate ways now ay. Thanks for the tour and all the other times you have done some insane eerie shit while I have been on this island" I say, sounding sure of myself and sarcastic, but the tremor in my voice clearly exposes the fear I am trying to deny. "Look out for high winds and rough seas won't you", he bares his teeth to snarl at me, just like he did to my daughter when she cried on our first day here and I say my final words to him as I walk towards the cottage, "fuck you".

Chapter Twenty-Seven

There was something so alluring about the cottage, despite the trepidation I had felt, that has now been replaced with a sense of being summoned. Like I was going home. The closer I got the more I was being drawn in, but I had no intention to fight the feeling, I wanted to see it, I was desperate to be inside. I opened the door and as soon as I crossed the threshold into the building the feeling of excitement and willing had gone. I now felt trapped. There was gloom in the air and a wave of negativity swept over me. The cosy glow was replaced by a cold dim lit room. My fight or flight response was throbbing, imploring me to run. Just as I contemplated escaping the door slammed shut and I knew even if I tried it would be impossible to budge. I just have to accept my fate now. I think about my little girl and begin to tear up, what if I mess things up, what if she has to grow up without me? I quickly swipe those tears away. I need to be strong, for the exact same reason I am scared. I won't let her down. I won't stop until I find Lainya and reunite her with our pumpkin.

The walls have oil lanterns which burn suspiciously close to the ceiling beams without leaving so much as a small scorch mark. The flames dance in a synchronised fashion as if they were manufactured to do so, but they are definitely real flames. The floor has straw scattered all over it, easier to clean than a carpet, I guess. I read about them doing this in the olden days, 'rushes' I think it was called. There was no obvious smell to the place so I can't assume the straw is for livestock, but it seemed fresh, which tells me someone lives here. I hope they are friendly, I feel weak, and for the first time since Lainya went missing I am starving and all I can think about is food, so good I can almost smell it. All my favourite foods. I am so hungry. Maybe I could make a snack while I am here, and without any trepidation I walk through the next door hoping to be met by a table full of pizza and cheeseburgers. It was so dark, I could still smell food, but it was too dark to see anything, then as if reading my mind 2 small fireplaces adjacent to one and other in the room erupted with a magnificent roar, like a big bang fitting to start a universe, let there be light. And stood at the back of the room, there is someone else here, behind a cluttered desk full of paperwork and cooking utensils, there she was.

"Lainya! Oh my god Lainya, it's really you. It's really you. I knew it, I knew you weren't dead. Are you okay are you hurt? I've been looking for…"

"I'm fine"

She said it so matter of factly, almost with a hint of annoyance, like I had left the toilet seat up or something, regrettably it was a tone I was accustomed to. "Is there anyone else here? Are you safe? How did you…"

"I said, I'm fine".

"Sweetheart, I know you have probably been through something, but can you give me a bit more than, 'I'm fine please".

I step forwards. I get my wish and hear more from her than 'I'm fine'.

"Stay the fuck back, don't fucking come near me"

"Lainya?! Sweetheart?"

"Stop calling me sweetheart, and stop fucking calling Lainya, that is not my name".

"Right, I don't know what's happening here" maybe she has had a bad fall, hurt her head, maybe she's struggling with the emotional toll of the last few days, I can relate to that. If her experience on this island has been similar to or heaven forbid worse than mine then she must be confused and terrified, I know I am. I need to be calm and just say whatever to get us safely out of here. I will play along for now. "Okay, okay, let's just talk. What is your name?"

"Sylvia"

"Sylvia?" I could not hide the shock and confusion in voice, where on earth has that come from, she does not have a middle name and as far as I know nobody in her family goes by the name of Sylvia.

"Yes, Sylvia, I know it is old fashioned but that has always been my name. It didn't suit me as a baby, but I am growing into it".

"Right, Sylvia, do you know who I am?"

"Yes, of course!"

I smile and I feel a sense of relief. She has some confusion of self, but at least she recognises me, that should aid me with getting her the help she needs.

"I came here to escape you. But here you fucking are, as always!"

Oh, well the sense of relief is gone. Back to sadness.
"Lain...sorry, Sylvia. I am your husband. We are married.

We are here on holiday. If you could let me, come a little closer, I can show you photos from our wedding day".

"I told you to stay back, do not come near me. How did you even find me? I thought this would be the end of this bullshit. Why can't you just go away?"

"I am not leaving you here, and I hope one day you will thank me for that" I am utterly useless at this, and emotion is beginning to cloud my rational thinking, anxiety is heightening, I am beginning to panic. "What about our daughter? We have a little girl, surely you remember her?"

She scoffs, "you really are a sick fuck. Don't you ever attribute that thing to me ever again! That pumpkin you carry around, pretending it's a child, our child?! Listen, loon, I am not your wife, and we have not had a baby together. That pumpkin you carry around should be nothing more than Halloween decoration. Listen, I am sorry, you are clearly, clearly, mentally unwell. I do not know if you have had a breakdown, or if you have always been a nut case, but all this, all this stalking me needs to stop. It has been years! You've made my life hell. I have begged you to leave me alone, my father told you to leave me alone. Everywhere I turn, you are there. I thought I had finally gotten away from you.".

I snap, "Don't you dare talk about our baby like that! This is absurd, I am not your stalker, we dated, we got engaged, we got married, had a baby, and more recently we went on a holiday. And I do not know what the fuck has happened Lainya but please just fucking trust me, let's get out of here, please let me help you. We can go somewhere, and we can just talk and figure everything out" I then recall another piece to the puzzle, possibly because I felt the bruising on my jaw "The police are looking for you! We need to let them know you are okay".

I take a few steps forward, but hastily stop in my tracks, to my absolute disbelief she has pulled a gun and is aiming it right at my head. Considering all the bizarre things on this island, this is the strangest thing that has happened? Is she going to tell me I have been married to a secret agent spy all this time?"

"Stop right there!" She holds the gun with such ease, so calm, she is not even shaking slightly. "You are not my husband, you are a very Ill man, and you have been stalking me and tormenting me for years. The police know that I am here, you shouldn't have been able to find me. You have two choices now, turn away and leave me the fuck alone, forever. Or you carry on this bullshit, and I fucking kill you. I don't want to do that, but I will, one way or another it ends tonight, please don't make me shoot you, just walk away".

"I am not a stalker, I am your husband, please just calm down and let me help you".

"Anytime I go anywhere you are there lagging behind, you turn up outside my work, you broke into my house, you turned up at fucking dad's funeral. You have been a living nightmare, please Nathan, please just walk away".

"This, this is insane. Please, just let me help you, I can't just leave you here, please I am begging you just let me help you, we will get through this together, I can't just leave you here". I place both my hands up in the air to show her I am no threat. I look her in the eyes hoping it will help her rekindle some memories of us, of her. There is a tear rolling down my cheek, it is leap of faith time "I know you don't want to hurt me, and you know I would never do anything to hurt you" I take a step forward and I see her finger pull on the trigger...

HER STORY

Chapter 1

I have not tried to disappear before though I have often considered it. In the modern world it is very difficult to achieve such. See, you can get rid of your mobile phone, your bank cards, credit cards, car, all your personal belongings, obtain fake IDs, and still be traceable because every city, motorway, shop and more have surveillance cameras, not to mention mobile phones again, everyone with a phone can capture your whereabouts, even if by chance. There only needs to be a 'reported sighting' of you in a general area at a general time and you can be tracked and traced from there and found, probably, that same day. It certainly has benefits, such as preventing crime or capturing criminals. The negatives, however, are for those of us that want to be left alone. I guess plastic surgery is an option, change of name, change of face, gain weight, lose weight, but that seems a heavy price for freedom. So, while I cannot simply disappear, I am thinking I can escape, I am going to be more like the great Houdini and less Machiavelli the prince.

Nathan has been in my life for 5, nearing 6 years, I have been stalked by him for all but 3 months of that time. The first 3 months he had potential to be a partner, maybe, but when you notice things like someone walking past your house for the 4th time in one evening, or they just having a habit for turning up wherever you are, it begins to suffocate you, by the 7th month of him 'being in my life' just the sight of him made my skin crawl, made me claustrophobic. So, that brings me to my current thinking. Time to escape.

I have no interest in being a victim, and I say that with all respect to other victims out there in the world. None of us wanted our lives to go in this direction. For me, the absolute worst part of being stalked by some entitled, obsessive, degenerate is the fact that I am now just a character of someone else's story. Imagine that being what your life is filtered down to.

I used to really enjoy murder documentaries until some of the exhibited behaviours of murderers became a bit close to home. If Nathan killed me, all the news stories and all of the documentaries would be centred around the murderer. What made him this way, what did he do, how did he get rid of the body. My part in all this, a prop, a name, but not a person. They would probably make him infamous by giving him a super cool name 'The Cold Coffee Shop Killer', also known as 'The Frappe'. I would be downgraded to 'victim'.

Some argue that I should not have to give up my life, and they are right, considering that I have done nothing wrong. But everything I have and everything I have built here in Sheffield is tarnished, all because he has a 'habit' of turning up wherever I am. Every memory of the last 9 years is one of fear, so forgive me if I am keen to move away. I know I shouldn't have to give this up, but I want to. In fact, I am desperate to.

He even turned up at my father's funeral. I foolishly expected he would have some level of decency and exhibit a level of respect for human life. But as i barely held my composure I looked around the room, and there he was, stood at the back, staring at me, almost shocked that I was disgusted he was there. That was the moment I knew my time in Sheffield was up. My career was finished, and my mortgage was switched to a buy-to-let mortgage, that particular detail was not difficult to give up.

I began conducting my research, firstly to find out about remote locations, my preference was for them to be holiday destinations so that my route there was easy. I had no experience of travelling alone. I knew that once I have accomplished that a few times then I could begin moving to different geographical areas that may not be as straight forward to access. I dipped into chat rooms online, I used them sparsely, and I found that the people who were on chat rooms a lot seemed to be looking for something specific that the real world was not providing them, such as companionship, an ear to listen, or a place to vent. I was initially apprehensive, I thought that knowing my luck I would have gained a few more stalkers.

I learnt of a place called Melas where you fly out to Greece and from there get a boat across to the tiny island. It is accessible but not well known, it is just a small dot on the map, it sounded perfect. There were murmurings online that it was haunted, it was for 'extreme tourists' and it was easy to disappear there. It ticked all the boxes.

I sold the majority of my belongings, I left the furniture in my home, it is more appealing to potential tenants to move to a partially furnished property, and the income from renting my house is going to be my only source of income until I can figure something out. A chunk of that monthly income is going to be shared between the estate agents and the mortgage provider. When I finally arrive in Melas I will have to be savvy with my spending, but much like the moving around it will be good life experience.

Chapter 2

Getting through the airport was not a straightforward as it should have been and I was delayed due to my 'suspicious behaviour', which I find is another insult to all victims out there. I was nervous, as I always was when I left the house. So, wherever there were a cue or slight hold up, or even when entering the next stage of check-in, I looked around and over my shoulder constantly hoping and praying he would not turn up. I explained to airport security that I was a little jumpy as I have a stalker, they initially mistook that as misplaced arrogance on my part but once they spoke to the police, they understood things have happened in the past and I was not making this up.

As things relaxed and I felt comfortable in the situation the verbal diarrhoea began "honestly, just going on holiday alone is a massive shift from my comfort zone, I have no desire to hijack a plane" and there it was, those final 3 words that kept me in that small windowless room right up until departure time. Once airport security and staff were satisfied, I was not a terrorist I was allowed to board my flight. Once on the plane, the stewardess' looked at me in such a way that I knew any sudden movement on my part would see me tackled to the ground and restrained. I'll need to remember to not go to the bathroom with any enthusiasm. The whole process thus far has been very stressful, and embarrassing even more so, with that, I ordered a few glasses of bubbly and allowed myself a nap, much to the relief of the flight crew, I am sure.

The final stage of the journey was to get a boat from the airport across to the island, it was very reminiscent of when I visited Venice with my parents when I was younger. The difference is that this island does have cars on it. And there was an option to get a coach through an 8-mile tunnel which runs underground. However, being in an undersea tunnel for that amount of time would make me feel much too claustrophobic. Also, it is the more expensive mode of transport to the island where the Melas council are very serious about lowering their carbon emissions. So, while you can use a vehicle, it will cost you.

I sat at the front of the boat. While I am extremely uncomfortable having people behind me, for obvious reasons, I do enjoy being at the front and pretending that I am navigating the boat, I have learnt through the years to give myself a sense of control wherever possible, just so I feel like my life is mine. I afforded myself a smile as I watched the blue blanket of sea in front of me ripple like a tossed duvet. Nearly there, the new beginning of a life that is all mine, where I am the main character and I decide the narrative.

People started to board the boat and take their seats as we were nearing the designated sail time. There was a bit of commotion towards the back of the boat, not enough to make me turnaround, it just sounded like a slightly clumsy person trying to negotiate a lot of luggage. Then the whispers began. I heard a lot of mentions of "pumpkin" "is that a pumpkin in that pram?" And I knew instantly. Nathan was here, he had found me, I wasn't free.

I turned my head slightly hoping my peripheral vision would be able to scan enough of the rear view to give me an idea of what is happening without me fully turning my head. But I did turn my head and what I saw was Nathan strapping a pram into the designated baby area of the boat, along with a bright pink travel case, he then looked directly at me, he smiled and gave me a limp wave and then went and sat down. I noticed he had a travel Sickness band on his wrists. Light purple with a slight rip around the button. I once wore these. I had experimented with the idea that if he saw me wearing them, he might think I was pregnant and perhaps leave me alone or at least give me some distance. It did not work even a little. So, they ended up in the bin. What I didn't know until now was that he had retrieved them from my bin.

I wonder how long he's been wearing them. That was at least a year ago. I felt sick. And not in a way that anti-sickness bands could relieve.

After my very brief fling with freedom, I have reverted to just become a character in someone else's story. 'The stalker would rummage through the victims bins to retrieve items and clothing she had thrown away, he would then wear them' creepy. At least my narrative hasn't changed. Get to the island and disappear.

If he had hoped to be a low-key stalker on this trip that idea has already failed miserably as everyone on the boat sat in stunned silence and horror as he was seasick all over the place. We sit for the last few minutes of the trip in a mess and stench he has created. Rather symbolic of the last 9 years of my life.

Chapter 3

I had been in communication with people on the island for quite a few months now. They are very secretive, I do not know their names or what they look like but that is the gamble with the internet anyway, many people aren't who they say they are. Sometimes for bad reasons, other times for reasons similar to mine. They were the first stage of my escape route and that was all I needed them to be. They had sent me a SIM card in the post because my mobile network would be redundant out here and they had arranged for a car to be available for me. Of course, I am sceptical of why complete strangers would be so helpful. I am hoping they are empaths who genuinely want to help me out.

I instantly felt a connection with this island, the sea air, the mountains it is just as I have pictured it. And the caves, they are just as I had dreamed about. Once I noticed the detail of the caves in the hillside a small sense of dread came over me and I could feel panic rising through my body, but as quickly as it started it went away and I snapped out of it. That was my old life, this is my new life. I looked back at the caves once more just to prove to myself that I wasn't scared and then I proceeded forward.

Nathan was behind me in the crowed of people disembarking the boat. He was peeling off his shoes and socks and depositing them in the bin. He is so vile. A small part of me wanted to confront him and ask him why he was here. Why won't he just let me vanish. But I have learnt that any small interaction I have with him just gives him the impotence to carry on stalking me, like in his mind he has made some sort of progress.

I extracted my mobile phone from my pocket and noticed a text was already awaiting me. It was 2 picture messages. One of a car and one of its location on the island, past the harbour, near the beach. It did not appear to be in a car park, in fact it looked rather abandoned. But it should be easy to locate.

I decided now that I had arrived at Melas, I would give these new friends of mine a quick phone call. I could sense Nathan watching me while I held the phone to my ear, good, I don't want him to know I am alone. I tapped the call symbol on my phone and straight away it made a strange tone followed with "number not recognised" I looked at the texts again, swiped the call button and got the same result. Impossible, how can I receive texts from this number but not make a call to it? Just then another text came through, all it said was 'keys under the passenger seat' I was halfway through texting a response when a final text appeared that said 'we hope we have been able to help you. Good luck'. Well, that is that then. No new friends, just good Samaritans assisting someone in need. Abrupt, strange, and slightly unnerving. But it has offered me a way out none the less.

I noticed that Nathan has veered off and this gives me a bit of breathing space. It is so eerie that he is so confidant in his ability to find me again that he goes about his everyday life before once again locating me. I do not know how he does it. I once had a selection of my everyday items checked for bugs that he might have planted on me when I had the misfortune of being in the same cafe as him but everything came back as clean.

I strolled by the pier, there was something so enticing about the boats and the ocean that seemed symbolic of freedom, and I instantly felt that I had made the right decision. I leaned on the railings which were unusually cold to say how hot the climate is out here. I looked down at the harbour at the shallow tide, I watched as the Sea Bream inspected the anchorage of the private sail boats and easily fell into the trance of watching them effortlessly glide through the salt water, I find there is something really therapeutic about watching fish locomotion.

I noticed my own reflection rippling and deforming like it was in a fun house mirror as the sun bounced off the surface of the water and rained diamonds down on me. I looked deeper at myself as something caught my eye and I let out a gasp like I had been winded, I could see in the reflection of the water that there was two people either side of me, stood very close and looking into the low tide as I was. To my left was a female in a long black cloak and to my right was an old looking gentleman, the gentle current made it difficult to distinguish anymore details than that.

I turned around quickly and gasped again as nobody was there, I turned and looked back at the water and the only reflection was mine. It must have been my mind playing tricks me, surely that is all it could be, a side effect of the years of torment I had endured. An elderly tourist walked past me sipping a bottle of water and gave me a reassuring smile, almost as if to ask me if I was okay as she walked past, I smiled back, again, I hoped this smile confirmed I was fine.

I had a little trouble shaking off the image of the 2 bodies that haunted my reflection, I understand they were not actually there but equally it looked so real, I wonder what it was I saw. Maybe it was a coincidence, and something was flying over me in the sky and my brain was trying to quickly adjust to what was happening tried to give the objects a familiar form. I don't know, not to worry, nothing bad has happened, hopefully I can start my life without having a mental breakdown. While It is devastating that Nathan is here, at least I actually have a plan to disappear and one I intend top follow through. The fact that he is here could work in my favour, maybe the realisation that I have disappeared will hit him harder and he will have no choice but to accept it and deal with it, and dare I say it, move on!

I strolled back along the harbour and I noticed there was an ice cream stand that was handing out free samples of new flavours , a quick glance of the shop window behind the cart informed me that this was an 'Ice Cream Relaunch – 14 new flavours', I do like Ice Cream but I have to say this new flavours hype was a slight exaggeration, like there was Coffee flavoured Ice Cream and then there was 'Expresso' flavoured Ice Cream which one would assume is just the same, just slightly stronger. But I can't complain, whatever helps them stay in business, and there is still a decent enough variety. I asked for a free sample of their strawberry Ice Cream but the man on the cart managed to entice me into trying their new Strawberry and Cream Ice Cream, from which I was convinced to purchase a two-scoop tub. I took refuge on a grass curb under a tall tree which provided shade and enjoyed my desert.

I then recycled the empty carton into the appropriate bin by the harbour railings and let out a groan as the bin was filled with maggots, feeding on discarded scraps.

Chapter 4

This was the first time in the last decade that I had not approached something with trepidation bit I did not feel brave, I felt desperate. Being stalked by Nathan took its toll on me. Early on it was just basic decision making, such as should I leave the house tonight, should I turn the lights on or off in my home and over thinking what impression that gives off from the outside. Soon enough, all decisions became too difficult to make, will I have a starter or go straight for a main, I even began making decisions I did not want to make on the basis that it wouldn't attract more attention.

I used to love a cold pint whenever I was in a pub or restaurant but the number of men that would comment on it began to really get on my nerves. Some would say something condescending thinking it was a complement like "lady with a pint, good lass" others would give me their unasked-for opinion "I find it a turn off seeing a lady with a pint. You should have a wine, or a gin and tonic". In my youth I could brush it off, sometimes tell them to fuck off. But like I say, once Nathan entered my life, any and all attention was not welcomed. Plus, if I am being honest, they never had a right to comment on me or what I was drinking anyway.

This time it is different, I am different, and I am determined to be free. The excitement I am feeling now can only be rivalled by that feeling you get on Christmas Eve as a child. I approach the walkway to the beach; a series of steps will elevate me to the sand dunes but according to the little map I received via text, before I begin the descent to the beach, I need to take a less obvious path which is where my escape vehicle awaits me. I have a quick look at the messages I received to remind myself of what I am looking for. All the texts have vanished? Strange because I do not remember deleting them. Oh, well, I can figure it out.

It is certainly a lot of steps, but I am not complaining, the road to freedom has been 10 years, what is a few steps now. Not to mention my escape has been planned out and arranged purely by the kindness of strangers, which I am still very uncomfortable with, but drastic times call for drastic measures, I tell myself I am grateful. The biggest lesson I am going to have to relearn is trust, trusting people. This may not be the best place to start such. But desperation is labelled so for a reason.

I only had to climb a few steps before I realise this island was haunted, or more specifically I was, because there he was. I had clocked him in my peripheral vision and granted myself a quick glance to be sure, and my living nightmare had entered the scene. Nathan had found me as always. He is a fair distance behind because he is dragging that pram with the pumpkin inside of it. He shouts a few things towards me as if to make out this was a planned rendezvous, but I do not acknowledge it, that would be a mistake. when we are alone in a secluded area like this, I get the creeps. I look ahead and power through.

He continues to shout over to me, something about how many steps there are, I maintain fixated on the task at hand, do not react keep moving forward. On a petty level I hate the fact that he is right, this is an unaccommodating quantity of steps. I am lucky that there is a significant distance between us in which I am confident that when the time comes to peel off to the right and collect my vehicle Nathan will be none the wiser, although it is a false confidence. I am concerned that him just being close by has the potential to mess things up. Which would be typical of him.

I hear a muffled sound coming from behind me and instinctively look over my shoulder, Nathen looks doubled over in pain by the pram. I do not know what has happened, but I hope it hurts. I now walk with a bit more intensity, considering the decent distance already between us, this is an opportunity for me to get out of sight. I am conscious not to run or jog as I fear that would invite a chase, but I am now power walking to freedom, which is some feat considering I am in flip flops and wading through sand.

After more power walking than I have the fitness to endure I am happy to see I am reaching my first check point, and even better than that I am looking around and I can't see Nathan anywhere. He must be really committed to dragging that pram through the sand. I briefly consider what illness he must have before swiftly shaking the thought out of my head. If there is anyone more underserving of my sympathy or empathy than him then I hope, we never meet.

There are two parts of the path that veer off to the right and seem to have a natural, yet manmade path in the sense that all the long grass is crushed down and has become a trampled walkway. I am almost certain it is the second right turn I need to take but my decision-making skills have become jaded, I really wish my phone had some details of all this for me to just glance at. I decided to trust my gut and go with the second right, I took a few more steps and then heard a strange low growl, it did not sound like an animal, more like a human trying to make an animal sound, but convincingly, I looked around and the air escaped my lungs as I fell back gasping, covering my mouth with my hand.

I wanted to scream, but I did not want to encourage a rescue attempt from Nathan, so I just froze. There was this, creature, I think, on its hindlegs it forms a tall physique that was a perfect silhouette in the sun, it then fell to all fours, to reveal more of its features, a huge cat, hairless with wide gaping eyes that were all black, its frame was like a puma but there was something so human about its face.

The longer I looked into its soulless eyes, and drowning in an abyss of darkness, the more I could feel my eyes widening in terror. It then broke eye contact with me and began to run down the first right turn, I could have sworn it hissed and said "Sylvia" but surely that is my imagination, surely. It could be something to do with all the travelling and then acclimatising to the heat here maybe.

Now I must think quickly, I do not know if that thing was a warning or if it wanted me to follow it or something, but it felt like it could have served as an omen of sorts, if there are such things. What I do know is that I have zero desire to follow it, so I am going to take the second right and hope it wasn't some sort of warning to me. I realise this frightening exchange has eaten up some time and I am determined to not let Nathan and his pumpkin catch up to me, so I kick off my flip flops and run as fast as I can until finally, I see the car awaiting me, exactly as I recall it in the photo I was sent. My heart is racing, a mixture of seeing some awful creature and the adrenaline of this plan coming to fruition. Right then, here I go, I am about to head into the unknown, but at least it is driving away from a decade of torment.

I am sure that the risk will be worth the reward.

Chapter 5

I remember the first time I met Nathan, it was complete and utter fate, but not in the romantic sense, more like the wrong place at the wrong time. I had never had any interest in dating apps, so I did like the idea of being swept off my feet by a handsome stranger, but even then, it was going to take something special. I enjoyed my own company, I enjoyed the freedom of being alone, and I had a decent job, a lovely home with a disgusting mortgage, but I was surviving. At that stage of my life, it would have been quite a sacrifice to dedicate my time to someone else, and potentially start sharing my wardrobe space with them, so like a I say, it would have to be someone extra special for me to reduce my evening reading hours.

I did not even want a pet for the companionship because of the care they require, it would impact on my life too greatly, and I do not even mean that in a selfish way, because if I loved something, such as a dog, I would give up every spare second suffocating it with care and attention. Surplus to say Nathan is special, and he is not like other guys, but in every worst way you can fathom.

I had been going to the same café on Ecclesall road in Sheffield city centre for years, it was a place I would frequent when I was a University student so to pop into an old haunt on the way to work set me up well for the day, it kept me in touch with my youth, I could sit and have a drink while reminiscing and generally go to work in a good mood. Before this routine I had a different routine where I would set about 6 alarms on my phone, the 6th being the absolute 'get your ass out of bed bitch' alarm, had a glass of water while throwing on my blouse and skirt and then prey public transport did not destroy what was a solid plan.

It was a routine for the short term, as the years go by, you realise your body is not going to tolerate routines like that and so I began early mornings, breakfast, casual stroll to Eccy road for a cup of Tea, then into work, fresh and ready to face the day. I did try to get up even earlier and introduce yoga into my routine, but I am not very flexible to say the least, and ultimately, it just seemed a dumb way to die.

This one particular morning I was standing in line studying the menu like I do every morning, knowing I will make the same order that I do every morning. I have never enjoyed being a people watcher, people do not interest me, so I would rather read while I wait, even though it was a menu that only altered seasonally. My attention was drawn to a clatter across the Café as a poor employee had the embarrassment of dropping their tray which caused a few of the mugs to smash. I let out a fed-up sigh as some generic imbecile shouted 'whhheeeeyyyyy' and it was at the moment I noticed Nathan, staring at me, slightly a gawk.

It feels strange to admit this now but when I first saw him, I did think he was attractive, there was something cute about him, a vulnerability of someone trying their best to be a grown up but not quite ready for life. He darted off to the bathroom, I assume to freshen up, he looked like he had slept on a bench. There is only so much a suit can disguise. Especially a cheap one.

Time past and I had my Tea and was having a quick look through work emails on my phone, it marginalises the impact of logging on at work if I have a rough idea of what was awaiting me. I knew Nathan was looking at me from time to time, trying his best to be discreet, some men will just stare at you and make you feel intimidated, others will casually glance in your direction, hoping you do not notice them.

My day was instantly thwarted as I noticed my mobile phone battery had died, I had a quick rummage through my handbag and realised I had not packed a charging cable, this means I was off the grid until lunchtime at the earliest, and I hate that. It was then I realised Nathan was walking towards me, not me directly but towards my direction, presumably to the exit, he smiled when he noticed me looking at him, I quickly looked away, frustrated that I had no connection to the Internet and no concept of time anymore. He walked past me towards the door before I blurted out "do you have the time?".

He initially looked flabbergasted but pleasantly surprised that I had spoken to him. Then things got slightly strange, he smiled at me and said "sure". I then sat there as he pulled out the chair opposite me at the table and sat down. I did not like the fact that he saw such an innocent question and turned into an opportunity, I was curious as to what the time was, so I encouraged him to tell me "Well?" He looked confused and spaced out, like there was an inner monologue running through his mind. He simply replied "well, indeed". What the hell is that supposed to mean, why can't men just talk to women normally?

I had grown tired of this interaction so tutted to imply such and repeated, "do you have the time?". He looked like he had been caught out and just repeated my question, "you want the time?", he then glanced at his wrist, looking sad that no watch was there and said, "Um, no, I don't have the time". This was tedious, I should have ignored him until he went away but instead, I fell to curiosity "Right…so, um, why did you sit down?" he replied, "I thought you said, got time? like you wanted to talk or something." Unbelievable, I had to address this stupidity, "But I don't know you! Wouldn't that be weird?" "I guess so, yes".

This is the exact moment I wish I could rewind and do over, wash over the mistake. But I admit, I felt sorry for him, and he did seem harmless, and as afore mentioned quite cute. What I should have said is something like "okay, well this has been a mix up, you can leave" or maybe just sat in silence until he left. Maybe I could have gathered up my belongings and exited and left him there, but instead I said "my name is Sylvia, what's your name?"

Chapter 6

I sat in the car seat and let out a deep sigh of relief, a tear rolled down my cheek, but I do not know it if is there because through a sense of relief or If I am still shaken by that bizarre creature I saw. I will figure out what the rogue tear was a tribute to later, but currently I am aware that I probably have a 10-minute window to drive off without Nathan seeing me. I very much doubt he would suspect me even if he saw a blonde in car from a distance, but it is not something I wanted to leave to chance.

I sat looking for the ignition in the car, there was nothing. I have never been in a car this modern before; how do I turn this bastard on? I fleetingly consider shouting "car on!" before repressing that stupidity. I was telling myself to stay calm, rushing and panicking is not going to help me figure this out, but what if Nathan is coming? He's not, stop that.

I pulled down the visor and a card dropped down, slapping me on the bridge of my nose. There was a slot for the card just above the gear stick, fancy, I inserted the card and a red button flashed, it read 'Engine ON/OFF' now it is getting simple. I pushed the button and shuffled in my seat to get comfortable. The engine still hadn't started, what is this witchcraft? Why won't this bloody thing start, I kicked out the foot pedals in frustration and the clutch being the outlet of anger worked, the dashboard lit up and the engine began to hum gently.

The sat nav turned on with a destination already set up, against my better judgement I decided I would see where it takes me. I have come this far, and my gut feeling is that this is the lesser of two dangers. The destination was pinned as 15 miles from my location and according to the dashboard I have 20 miles worth of fuel, this leaves me with very little margin of error, and adds to the sense of reluctance which I have been working so hard to push to the back of my mind. Maybe I am being too cynical, perhaps there is a petrol station at this destination.

Five miles into my journey and an ease is coming over me, not only is this car a fantastic drive but the scenery is quite simply breath taking, and with such beauty to behold it is quite easy to forget your problems momentarily and relax. I was so at ease I decided to further explore the digital wizardry of this vehicle and turn on the radio to take in some of the local culture, I hope they don't just play English music, surely not. There was some static as if it was searching for the right radio waves before it went silent and the digital screen turned off, which put an end to the culture dive rather abruptly.

I noticed the screen light up again as I was navigating a harsh corner into a lush hillside when the frequency of the radio began to skip at a tremendous pace, I pushed the power button a few times to try to cancel the radio, but eventually relented, it was not a big deal, then suddenly an incredibly loud blood curdling scream burst through the car speaker, causing it to crackle as the audio broke the buffer, it lasted, maybe five seconds, causing me to skid and swerve such was the sudden volume and distressing sound. It stopped suddenly and only normal traffic noise remained. I pulled over as my heart was racing and I was alarmed.

I gripped the steering wheel really tight, as if it was the only thing that would protect me, it was the only object that offered me some stability and control, I slowly pulled up the handbrake and took deep breaths, I rested my forehead on the steering wheel without relenting my grip. I was startled, but also spooked, that scream is the most frightening sound I ever heard, and I cannot understand why it happened, what caused it. As I was trying to rationalise what I had just experienced, an ice cold snake coiled around my spine and caused a sense of dread to rattle my bones, I sensed there was someone behind me on the backseat of the car, my mind instantly flashed back to when I was stood on the pier and there were two people stood behind me as I awoke from the trance the ocean had put me in. I had successfully brushed it off and told myself it was just a trick my mind was playing on me. But I know what I saw. I knew I had to move away from the steering wheel at some stage, I could just glance up and look in the rear-view mirror and if there's someone sat behind me, I could quickly dart out of the car and flag some help perhaps.

I count to five and then look into the rear view mirror, my heart is racing so hard that I can feel the veins in my neck pulsating and a cardiac rhythm thumps in my ear drums, the back seat is empty, with that slight relief I feel braver and spin around to check that these backseat phantoms had not suddenly ducked under their seats or something equally ludicrous but I can confirm I am alone in this car.

The ice-cold chill in my body begins to thaw out as I breathe and let out a muffled chuckle to myself. I need to calm down.

I carry on following the Sat Nav, it is quite a rarity driving here where there is not many cars to contend with, if this was back home I imagine it would be gridlocked traffic by now. Here I can almost afford to be careless. I glance over at the sat nav and it says I am about two miles away from the pinpoint destination. My adrenaline is now causing my chest and temples to throb. I can do 50 on this particular stretch along the coast so I will be at there in no time, wherever 'there' may be. I look along the sea stretching out and see a picturesque lighthouse in the far distance, I must say that parts of this island are idyllic.

There is a disturbance in the long grass which run parallel with the road, I slow down slightly as I attempt to determine what it may be. To my disbelief it is the creature from earlier, galloping on all fours at a tremendous speed, it is running in line with the car, its body looks like pure muscle as I can see from the cardio the inner facets at work. I catch a glimpse of it leading galloping legs and notice it has hands where I would expect paws to be. What the hell is this thing? It looks over in my direction, its almost human face, sharp teeth, and long lips, but a human nose and eyes, like its features had been drawn by a child.

The creature was able to keep up with the car even when I attempted to lose it by going up to 60 mph. Over the roar of the engine, I can hear its fast breathing, harsh, fast, and moist. What is this animal? It makes direct eye contact with me and smiles, I feel nauseated, it then thrust its whole body into the side of the car causing me to lose control and skid, the car is spinning across two lanes and just before I can make sense of what is happening an airbag inflates into my face saving my nose from exploding on the steering wheel, through the corner of my eye I can see a wall which is presumably what halted my acceleration.

Chapter 7

There was a period in my life, let's call it a blip, where I actually considered for a split second that Nathan might be boyfriend material. He was certainly keen, well keen was how it came across, you never know what someone is internalising, I guess keen developed into obsession, and that is how he went from potential boyfriend to someone who ruined the last decade. I won't ever get that time back, but as long as I continue to try and make up for it, I will know he hasn't taken everything from me. He won't win.

The early morning 'dates' were something I just fell into, every time I arrived, as per my routine, he was already sat there with my drink ready for me. And having spent most nights with a glass of wine and a good book, it was pleasant to have a bit of human interaction in the mornings, it helped warm me up before I had to exchange small talk with the people, I am forced to spend the majority of my week with, otherwise known as work colleagues.

I reluctantly admit, even though it seems ridiculous now, there was something nice about the way his eyes lit up when he saw me, every morning I left that Café I genuinely felt like I had made his day. And that is not arrogance on my part, rather that is the vibe he gave off.

The morning, I remember most is when things started to change for the worst, that obviously sticks out in my mind. I knew he fancied me, he paid for my drink every morning for a start, he was very sketchy about his data analysis skills so from that I assumed he did not have a job but wanted to impress me, which did seem cute without the clarity that comes from hindsight.

On this morning I was running late, and nearly decided to skip the morning brew altogether, but as fate dictated, I decided a bit of company was required, dare I say I regarded him as a friendly face back then. I was running late because I was having a reoccurring nightmare and when my alarm went off that morning, I just closed it down and must have fell straight back to sleep. The amount this nightmare was impacting my sleep had caused me to be careless and I had neglected to plug my phone in to charge that night.

Such a comedy of errors is never a good way to start a day. I threw on the same clothes as I had worn the day before as they were scrunched up on the bedroom floor, I put my hair in a bobble and grabbed my bag and was out the house within a five-minute period. I think I looked like shit that day, and that is not something I say hoping that people will correct me, I am not a fish for compliments kind of woman, I would rather just blend in with the room, but I do like to look a certain level of pretty, just for me. Make up is not always required but on this day with all the rushing and sleep deprivation I dare say a thin layer of foundation would have helped.

So, I rushed into the café, he looked relived to see me, like he was genuinely worried I was not going to turn up, which I should have seen as a red flag, and I mentioned to him I'd had a 'mad dash' to get out the house and needed the toilet. I dropped down my bag and a few of my possessions fell out, a few pens, my work schedule, business cards and probably some chewing gum and small perfume bottle.

I noticed these belongings spill out, but, and again to hate to admit this, I felt at ease around him, so I decided to pee first and tidy up second. When I came back, I noticed my possessions had clearly been looked through as the pile had been disturbed, a second red flag in seven minutes. I decided to tell him more about why I was rushing and about the nightmares I had been having, I felt if I spoke about them, I may not feel so troubled by them.

So, I explained the caves, which now I know are eerily reminiscent of the hillsides on this island, I explained the strange people muttering with their backs to me, only for some disturbance to alert them to my being there, how real it felt, and how they knew my name. Just remembering those nightmares now makes me shudder.

He hung on my every word, like a child having a bedtime story, I got the sense that he felt I was really opening up to him, like this was a development in our relationship, when really, I was just trying to make sense of the nonsense I had been dreaming.

"Damn"

"I know, it's stupid".

"No, it is not, it sounds scary. Do you need support? I could sleep on the couch, nothing weird?"

"Um, no, thank you. No. Erm…"

"Nah, it's fine, just offering, so how often is this happening?"

"I don't know a few times a week maybe".

"I wonder what it means. Maybe you're eating too much cheese before bed".

He waited for me to laugh, I just looked back at him, coming here was a mistake today, he is not helping, I have shown a slight vulnerability, and he is trying to capitalise.

"Sorry, that was a stupid joke, this isn't funny. I would be creeped out. That is why I was saying if you ever need any company…"

By this stage I had heard enough, "well, time for work, thanks for the brew".

I gathered my things and left, Nathan initially looked disappointed at my abrupt departure, but then was lost deep in thought. I think, although I cannot be sure, that it was this train of thought that he had clearly just boarded that was the beginning of my real nightmare. Judging by the following actions I am pretty certain that is the case.

I finished work that day at 5.15 and was talking to my colleague about what her weekend plans are and other convincing small talk that means we don't have to walk down the staircase in awkward silence. As we walked down the drive from the building, I clocked Nathan standing across the road with a bunch of flowers. I felt sick. Yes, I thought he was cute, and I did not mind the routine we had fallen into of sharing a table in the café, but I had always knocked back his advances so that he knew where he stood, at least that was what I thought.

I was shook that he had turned up outside my work, I found it so creepy. I assume my spilt belongings had been shuffled about that morning because he had a look at my business card, not the biggest crime, but certainly careless on my part. My colleague looked across at Nathan then at me, I gave her a look to say do not leave me, she gave an uncertain smile which told me she doesn't know the context but perfectly understands the assignment.

As we approached Nathan, he looked taken back that I had someone with me, but he quickly tried to relax into the situation

"Oh hi, this is awkward, I'm here waiting for a date".

"Funny"

"I was going for playful. Look, I'm not a psychologist, I don't know what your dreams mean but my dream is quite simple, let me take you on a date".

I could not believe this was happening, I was so certain that we were secured in the friend zone, and even that is at a push, if I had to clearly define it, I would say we are two strangers that drink at the same café each morning and pass the time with a chat. I knew he fancied me, but I also know I made it clear I was not interested.

"Look Nathan, I do not think of you in a romantic way, I am sorry, plus…" I linked arms with my colleague "we are about to get some tea together" she looked bewildered before smiling and nodding, proving all those years of GCSE Drama were a complete waste of her time.

Nathan replied "Okay, sounds great".

A strange response I thought at the time, in hindsight I assume he just heard what he wanted to hear, my colleague and I walked off and went to a restaurant down the road. I apologised for essentially taking away her evening but compensated her by paying for the food.

I will never forget the look on her face as I was chatting away and something caught her attention and she completely disengaged from me, and her eyes saw through me and then wondered across the room. I turned instantly to see what was wrong, what had spooked her so, and there was Nathan, pulling out a seat at a table directly across from ours. He had followed us here. And this, sadly, was the first of many, many occurrences.

Chapter 8

I slowly pealed my face away from the airbag, I knew I had to face this latest catastrophe at some stage, I did not want to give any passers by the impression I was badly hurt, a side from being a little shaken up I am absolutely fine. I scrape myself out of the drivers' seat to take a look at my handy work.

Right, lets tally up my experience so far, I came here to escape my stalker, said stalker stalked me to this island to continue his stalking, I was haunted by two disappearing people at the harbour, I have been stalked further by some bizarre looking wildlife that looks like a sketch of an animal with some human biology, and I have subsequently crashed my car into a wall which, judging by the way the bonnet has crumbled I would assume it is a write off. Not forgetting that this car was rented on my behalf by some kind people from a stalker support chat room. In terms of starting my new life, this has been a fucking disaster.

The Sat Nav is cracked and unreadable, but I recall there was not much further to go. I will have to go on foot for the rest of the journey, I sincerely hope that creature does not turn up again, I have nothing on me that could be used as a makeshift weapon. Since the accident there has been no cars or people go by, I am at a bit of a loss at what to do. And now it is eerily quiet. I grab the few belonging's I have and take the Key Card from the Car and decide to proceed, assuming there is someone to welcome me at the destination I can fill them in on what has happened, I just hope it will be obvious who I am and who they are, they will be expecting to see this car, and I do not know who or what I am looking for.

This stretch of walking did give me time to reflect and reach an inner peace, I reached a stage of serenity in which I was serenaded and carried by the calming soundscape of ocean waves. It is really odd that I have not seen another person for quite some time but equally I am happy to be off the beaten track and I am hoping to have the opportunity to indulge in a less touristy element of Melas. Sure, there has been some setbacks, namely crashing the car after being attacked by an animal but I am definitely well away from Nathan and that is what I came here to accomplish.

I reached an area of the Island where the cliff top lowers significantly so that it is just a small drop down to the beach below, I stood along the edge surveying the stretch of sand and still nobody was present, I should come back here one day, maybe buy a book and towel, I could set up for the day on my own area of personal, private, paradise. I decided to carry on my travels but stopped suddenly as I turned, and a little squeal escaped my throat.

There was an old man stood directly behind me, close enough that I could smell him, he smelt of fish and Iron and was wearing what appeared to be a very dated fisherman's outfit, he did not respond or react to my squeal. He just carried on staring straight ahead, just over my shoulder. I turned back quickly to see what he might be looking at, but everything was quiet and peaceful, even the waves seemed to glide across one another rather than crash and angrily foam. I decided to talk to him.

"Erm, Hi? Are you okay?" No response.

"Are you from this island? Only, I have crashed my car and…" he did not even break his stare, he just continued looking straight ahead.

"Are you a fisherman?" There was something so familiar about him, but I couldn't place it, I decided one more attempt at pleasantries before I awkwardly slunk away and left him standing there.

"So, umm, hi my name is Sylvia" as soon as I mentioned my name his eyes broke their stare and he looked directly at me, still not speaking but seemingly awoken from his trance. Had he been expecting me? I was about to continue talking when he began to clamp his jaw together and looked really angry, his fists were by his side, clenched and shaking. Keen to avoid any more disasters I took a few steps back and his stare returned to the ocean.

I noticed a single tear rolling down his right cheek and began to take a few steps back, at this he did not acknowledge my movement. I let out another gasp which thankfully did not break the apparent trance he was in, I remember why he looked so familiar, he was one of the people whose reflection stood behind me at the harbour. How had he managed to vanish. And why does he keep appearing around me?

"Who are you?" I blurt out and shock myself.

"Why won't you talk to me?" I say, more aggressively then intended. I guess my bullshit tolerance level is dwindling.

Again, he begins to grind his teeth into a snarl and his fist begins to clench so tight it turns white as he slowly turns towards me. I have no intention of standing my ground to evidence what transpires, and I simply run away as quick as I can. After about roughly 100 metres I glance back to see if the smelly fisherman is chasing me, he seems to have vanished once again. I standstill nervously cuddling myself and rubbing my arms, my blood has run cold, I feel like I must have just seen a ghost.

Chapter 9

The stalking began rather casually, we would bump into one and other in the supermarket and I would make sarcastic remarks such as "oh fancy seeing you here, what are the chances?" as if to say oh you're here at the exact same time as me at a supermarket that is not close to your home. I started to change my routine to try and get rid of him so I would try different supermarkets on different nights but more often than not he would appear and give me that fake puzzled look and claim we were like 'two peas in a pod'. Sometimes it was even more unnerving, he would just follow me down the aisle but try to not be seen, or he would walk quickly down to the bottom of an adjacent aisle and then just watch me intently.

On one occasion he was writing on a scrap of paper while watching me, and while I can't be sure, I think he was making a note of the items I shopped for. What reinforced my suspicion was that same night the following week I had a home delivery from a supermarket, one I did not order myself and it had my entire weekly shop correct. I sent it back of course, I had not ordered it and I had not paid for it, but I closed my door and locked it and then ran around the house locking all the doors and windows. He knew where I lived.

I had stopped going to the café in the mornings, I just afforded myself an extra half hour in bed as my change to routine. It would have been a silver lining had it not made me feel so trapped. The first person I told was my dad, a wonderful man and very protective of me. He told me that if I ever felt unsafe, I just had to ring him or text him saying 'I'll email you the spreadsheet' and then he would know I was in danger and would use the tracker on his phone to get to my location. This did make me feel slightly safer. Not to mention my dad was what I would class as a 'typical Sheffield bloke' old school and, basically just a fucking tough man. I would almost be worried for Nathans safety if my dad got a hold of him, I do not care for violence.

There were a few occasions where I thought I saw Nathan but instantly brushed it off like 'no surely not', I was either being silly or my brain was trying to protect me, but I was almost victim shaming myself. As the years went by, I would look back at these times and know it was him without a shadow of doubt and that I wasn't being silly. He would be on the bus I took to work sat at the back staring at me from the second I stepped on, to the second I stepped and cautiously looked back.

Some days he would be on the bus home from work too, I would sit there terrified that he would get off the same stop as me and offer to walk me home, or just follow me and try to force his way into my house. He never did either of those things, he would just watch me whenever he could. It perhaps was not terrifying, but it was immensely creepy.

He was once outside my work just feeding the pigeons while I was interpreting a fresh intake of results, I knew I would be finishing within the next 20 minutes, and I was frightened to go outside if he was going to be there still. I have always prided myself on being courageous and head strong but this whole ordeal had begun to break me down and forced me to retreat within myself. I wouldn't go places in case he would turn up but prior to this I was very sociable. I swallowed my pride and approached a male colleague who was particularly stocky and dare I say neanderthal looking.

"Hey"

"Hi, you okay"

"Um, no not really"

"Oh?"

"There's this guy" he instantly rolled his eyes, what a prick. "And I don't want to sound dramatic, but I think he is kind of stalking me"

"Right, what's he doing?"

"Well, he asked me out once and I said no, and now he keeps turning up everywhere I go and…"

"How did you meet him?"

"Just by chance in Café, we used to have a drink together every morning".

"Well bloody hell mate, there's no wonder he's an admirer, don't you think that was leading him on? What did you expect"?

"I expected I could have a conversation with someone of the opposite sex and it does not automatically mean I had to then go on a date with them. We were never dating, we never saw each other outside of that scenario, until recently anyway, but I was not leading him on".

"Why are you telling me this?"

I let out a deep sigh, and although I was frustrated with myself that did not prevent me from beginning to well up. "He's outside now, and I am scared, could you maybe walk out of work with me? I think he would leave me alone, if you did".

He got up and looked out of the window, "Is that him? Feeding the birds?"

"Yes, he's been there a while".

"He's not that bad looking to be fair to him. I expected him to be some greasy weasel looking bastard".

"So, you're saying I should be flattered? You know what, forget I asked anything, I will handle this on my own"?

"Fucking hell calm down will ya, I was just saying, look I will go down there now and tell him to bugger off".

"Thank you"

"And don't be too hard on the bloke ay? I'd stalk you as well if we didn't work together every day ha-ha, at least you're attractive enough to be stalked, some women would see it as a compliment".

I stood in stunned silence by what I had just heard coming from this moronic man, I looked down from the window as he menacingly strode towards Nathan, puffing his chest out and holding his arms aloft like he was carrying carpets. There was a brief exchange, then Nathan began to laugh, as did my colleague. They then shook hands and Nathan walked off and down the road while my colleague strode back towards the stairs like his bollocks had tripled in size.

We locked eyes as he returned to his desk, I looked at him expecting some form of update, he looked back at me puzzled.

"Well?"

"What?"

"For fucks sake, what happened?"

"He seemed alrate to be fair, he was just feeding the birds, says he is not stalking you, but he wouldn't turn you down. I said neither would I. I think you can relax, maybe don't fancy yourself so much".

I had heard enough, what is wrong with men? Disgusting pigs. I went into the toilet and locked myself in a cubicle to cry, not because I was, fragile, not because I was weak, but because if I hadn't, I would have beaten him to death with his laptop and kicked him off the top floor of the building.

Chapter 10

By rough estimation I think I have maybe have a mile left to navigate, my phone is utterly useless, but I keep it in my pocket for a reassurance that I'm not entirely cut off from the world, I am sure I will eventually get some signal. I only really need the Sat Nav, its not like I'm wanting to scroll social media, do a quick post to update my friends 'Met an angry fisherman had to run, was rate scared, LOL'. I deleted all that shit years ago anyway, any social media activity is an instant advantage to stalkers, potential stalkers, and exclusively perverts.

We live in a world where surviving cancer would get less 'likes' than a bikini photo. It is a sick world, what is happening to humans, are we all sick? Out evolved evolution and now the expectation is to mentally handle advancements beyond comprehension. AI can beat a world class chess champion in 19 moves. I stop myself there, I am distracting myself because of the uncertainty around what I am doing, I need to focus. I need to brave. Stop spiralling.

I embark upon what seems to be a more populated area of the island, there is a few holiday makers around and a few stalls set out selling fruit and offering hair braiding, a charming yet unexpected combination. Still, do whatever gets you paid; I am not knocking it. I stroll past a row of cute buildings, weathered looking with an unhealthy dollop of moss developing upon their straw roofs, the windowsills are crumbled and look like they would not even support the weight of a hanging basket.

All the small homes are dwarfed by the overarching leaning building with all its menace looking like it is trying to intimidate anyone who walks near its entrance. As I approach, I notice it is a pub, 'The Leaning Inn', well the name makes sense, the aesthetics do not, I would hate it 'inn' there. Outside of the pub are two men locked into a game of chess, their gaze turns from their game as I walked by, one of them still has a rook in his hand hovering across the board in suspended animation. If he plants his piece where it is currently hovering, I would be able to take his King in 7 moves. They both stare and do not relent the gawking even when I frown at them. Men can be such pervs.

I continued strolling casually looking for anyone who may be looking for me. It has certainly made things trickier that I do not know who or what I am looking for. I purchased a ham and egg salad sandwich from a randomly placed deli counter attached to a horse and carriage, situated by a fountain in the middle of what appeared to be a village square.

I ate it pretty quick; I did not realise how hungry I was but the mayonnaise I am wiping from my chin tells me I lacked a certain elegance while eating it. This get away mission has been quite an uncertain adrenaline ride so far; the stress of the day did not allow my stomach time to register its emptiness.

The further I continued forward the further I departed from the populated area of the island, and a sense of nerves began to creep in. The surroundings are beautiful, there is no doubt about that, but with such an environment the isolation ignites your survival instincts, sounds become creepier, movements become threatening, and your heartbeat has its own bass speaker located in your inner ear.

I had a pen in my pocket which I am now rotating round my fingers, it is a habit I have which is usually done to keep me engaged in boring meetings, which is pretty much 'all' meetings. I am doing it now as a comfort mechanism. My irrational brain is telling me it could also double up as a little weapon, my rationale brain is telling me that probably won't be needed.

A little black cat comes running over to me and started working its way around my legs like an infinity loop. It does not have a collar or bell, but its purring was a giveaway. I do love cats and this friendly little interaction makes me want to buy one. I kneel so I can really scratch behind its ears, it seems to love that, I am saying 'it' because I don't know if it is a boy cat or a girl cat. It climbs onto my lap and cuddles its head under my chin. This interaction continues before I remember I am in the middle of attempting a meet and greet and I need to continue before it becomes a search and rescue. I kiss the cat on its head as it further attempts to merge into face, it seems to really like me. Or maybe I still have some mayonnaise on my chin.

The cat grew bored of my affection and no doubt realised I had no food to give it and with that it hopped off my knees and began running towards a woodland area. Not a particularly inviting one either, I can't quite remember ever seeing such a neglected area, so vast and so unkept, it does not encourage picnics that is for sure. The trees are so thick I imagine it would make an excellent training area for lumberjacks. It is somewhat unsettling that the field of grass that leads up to the woodland area all looks dead as soon as you go over the fence, like there is a clear threshold crossing point. But why has it all browned? Looking at the thick, vastness of the Forrest I can imagine there is not a lack of nutrients in the soil. My knowledge of plants and growth do not exceed the stereotypical levels of a city slacker, so I am happy to accept that it seems odd, yet there is probably a good explanation as to why, and I do not need to know or understand.

I could see my lack of sense of direction had led me to a rather derelict area of the island and this is most likely not where I am supposed to end up so I decided to head back towards the centre, worst case scenario is I will have to turn back and walk this way but at least I will have the opportunity to purchase another sandwich. As I turned something made a swift move that was registered by my peripheral vision I looked back to the woodland area and there stood a person in a long black cloak.

I do not know how to explain what I am feeling but I know this is who I am here to meet, and I felt myself being drawn to them. I wish it was someone in a more friendly and accommodating guise but with each step towards them I began to feel safer, and warmer, any trepidation began to lift, and I began to feel like this was not just a new life for me, but rather this was my destiny. I was within arms reach when I said "I'm here" much to my own surprise.

I recoiled in disbelief as the person wearing the cloak turned around, blonde hair, green eyes, tiny scar on her chin, she is, but…that is, she's me?!

Chapter 11

It got to a point that I was so scared of Nathan that I went to the police. Unfortunately, this did not help matters, in fact, it made me feel much worse. There was one evening where I had been asleep in bed and it had been a stormy night, one of those storms that is so strong they give it a human name so that you can blame the destruction on something 'bloody storm Nigel blew my fence down' that kind of thing. I had left the small panel window in my bedroom open a little as always, I like there to be a gentle breeze on my face while the rest of my body is wrapped up and cosy from the neck down. Due to this storm, and I forget its name, there was loud whistling through the gap in my window, the rain and wind slapped the glass in a way reminiscent of going through a car wash. I scraped myself out of bed and shut the little window which muffled the whistling noise.

I open the curtain slightly to investigate the garden, I was hoping to catch a flash of lightning and to see how drastically the trees were rocking in the wind, there is a perverse pleasure in watching a storm when you are inside and cosy. The storm accommodated my wish though I wish it had not, there was that flash so bright that it lights up the whole estate as if it were 2 seconds of daylight before descending quickly back into the dead of night.

I thought I saw someone sat in my garden, just casually on the garden furniture, facing my house. I closed the gap in my curtain so that only my eye could peep through. It felt like another flash of lightning wasn't going to happen, but it did, and the garden furniture was empty. I considered for a split second that my mind was playing tricks on me, but I had a timely confirmation from another flash of lightning that revealed someone stood starring up at my bedroom window.

I stumbled back and threw my hand over my mouth to silence my scream, that was Nathan, just stood starring at my house. It was a stormy night, torrential rain, thunderstorm, the works, and was just stood there, soaking wet staring at my house. I was terrified. I remember my thoughts were racing as I considered how often has he done this? Why would he do it in this weather? Am I in danger?

The next morning, I reported this to the police, and they sent two officers around to talk to me and do a reccy of the house perimeter. I know it is cliché to say, and it is stating the obvious, but I will say that I am aware that not all police are bad, I do not know the facts and figures so I cannot comment if the majority or minority are good or bad, but I do know that some police are decent, moral, courageous and do their job. But as with any job there will be people who are self-serving arseholes, bullies, that can tarnish a good reputation. Both Policemen were courteous and professional when they arrived but once they were in the house and had a cup of tea and relaxed their badge must have fell off and their true selves reigned.

"Right then, tell us exactly what happened darling?"

"Darling?"

"Sorry about him, he meant sweetheart". They then grinned at each other. Idiots.

Sensing I did not like this attempt at humour they quickly changed back to a slightly more professional demeanour "We're just trying to lighten the mood, but listen we're here to help and it is important to us that you do feel safe, especially in your own home, so can you tell us what has been happening?"

I told them everything, how Nathan and I met, what had been happening and where I had seen him, and they nodded and took notes. I was wearing a vest top and had a zip-up gym hoodie on over that, after the 3rd time I clocked one of them looking at my breasts I zipped up my hoodie and they looked frustrated at that.

"Do you have any cameras around the house, doorbell, back garden, anything like that?"

"I don't, although I will buy some now".

"Good idea. What about your neighbours?"

"I don't know what their security set up is to be honest, it could be worth you asking them? I rarely speak to them".

"And you said you were in bed and saw him through your back window?"

"Yes, that is correct?"

"And you sleep in the backroom".

"Umm, yes?"

"Would you mind if I go up and take a look?"

"I would prefer you didn't. All that would confirm is that I sleep up there, which I have already told you".

"No problem. Really, that's fine. I hope that did not make you uncomfortable and I apologise if it did".

Sensing his partner was exposing himself as a pervert the other officer chimed in, "Look, there is not much we can do right now. As harsh as it sounds, as things stand, it is all your word against his. Now, that is not to say we do not believe you, we do, but in terms of getting some protection in place such as a restraining order we will need more evidence to support that. So, what I suggest is that if there's ever a time he is here again, or outside your work, or wherever, call the station, we'll have a record set up this afternoon and we'll be able to build a picture from there".

"Okay, that is fine, I appreciate you can't just spring to action off my sole account. I will look into getting some camera's up as well".

"Good idea".

They both stood up, the one who I had already silently named Officer Creep put his hand on my shoulder as if consoling me and then gave me a wink. Somewhat inappropriate. He said "oh and I'm sure your husband or boyfriend will want to beat the shit out of this guy, but it is best he leaves it to us" without thinking I said "I live alone" stupid mistake, or rather stupid society that means me saying something like that puts me in a potentially dangerous predicament.

The following evening there is a knock at my door, I…and I hate to admit this, crawl across the dining room floor on all fours and peep just above the windowsill to see who is at the front door, it's Officer Creep. I reluctantly open the door a creak.

"Hello"

"Hi, yeah, look I was just in the area and…"

I noticed he was not in his police uniform "are you off duty".

He raised an eyebrow and gave an arrogant smile "why yes, yes, I am"

"Then why are you here?"

"Like I said, I was in the area and just thought I would check up on you, check you're okay".

"I am fine thank you" I began to close the door and he put his foot onto the doorframe to prevent it from closing fully.

"Are you not going to invite me in? A woman in your position, alone, frightened, it would probably help you feel safe having a cop in the house, right?"

"Please move your foot".

With that his face turned stern, he looked to be clenching his jaw " listen, you think I go around every stupid bitch that needs help? Let. Me. In!"

I placed my foot and knee behind the door to further strengthen my hold on the door should he try to force it further but luckily for me a couple from up the road were strolling past the driveway walking their dog so I took my opportunity and said loudly, but not shouting "okay, you can leave now bye!" he had also clocked them and presumably did not want to draw attention to what was happening and relented his foot from the doorway. I quickly locked the door and ran into the dining room in time to see him storm off up the driveway.

Chapter 12

Fleetingly I considered if there might be some form of mirror at play, my brain instantly calling for the most rational explanation, but the person stood opposite me, the me opposite me, is dressed differently. I must be cracking up. I said "Hi" only to hear "Hi" said back to me simultaneously, my face, my body, my voice. What on earth is happening.

I move my right arm up, she mirrors it perfectly, how is this possible?! I put my left hand out to touch her and our hands touch in the same place, so she is real, we have touched I look up at her astonished, she also looks up at me astonished. I then go for the ultimate test, I decide to blurt out whatever springs to mind "purple, pants, cracked roof, watch, sink, books, stats…" we both say. We both share a little yet identical laugh at how ridiculous this is.

I take a step back, as does she, I run my fingers through my hair considering what to do next, my mind is racing, and I fear I am having a mental break down. Contrary to prior interaction, she breaks the mould and says "Follow me, quickly" she then turns and sprints into the woods. The more distance created between us the colder I feel, the more vulnerable I feel, so acting purely on instinct I shout "wait" and dart after her.

The forest is a harsh terrain, the overwhelming smell of the plant life makes it seem difficult to breathe, the tree branches above interweave like hands holding and locking fingers and the darkness this creates makes the air seem humid and damp. I will either die from lack of oxygen or drown here, but I need to catch up to me, she'll know what I am supposed to do next, she will keep me safe.

It is the strangest thing, there is no wind here, the atmosphere is too thick, but still it seems some of the tree branches move slightly, I have been slapped across the face 3 times already, although I am running and stumbling around, I assume the trees are not moving and relax that paranoia.

The version of me in front of me moves through the woodland with such grace and ease it is as if she is floating through. This is easily the strangest thing that has ever happened to me, stranger still is that I am not scared. I feel really calm; it feels right, like I am complete, like I finally belong.

'She me' was ahead of me by about 200 metres, and that is a very rough estimate. I have not run the 100-metre sprint since I was in secondary school, my record was 17 seconds back then. I do not know how quick I would be these days, not to mention that I am barefoot in a forest. So, while I do want to catch up to her and try and talk some more, I doubt my ability to get to her in under 35 seconds by which time she could have been spooked and run away from me, me being a maniac sprinting with muddy and bleeding feet just to say hello.

She appeared to be at a sort of crossroads, nothing that could be determined as a clear path, but there were trampled bushes and flowers that make it look so. She turned around to me and smiled. I wanted to kiss her. Wait, what?! No, I don't. Do I? She is beautiful, and it is narcissistic of me think that. I think I need some water and a sit down, that was a strange few seconds I just had. We stood a significant enough distance apart and it was as if time slowed, I had an expectation something was about to happen, but I do not know what, then she blew me a kiss. I did not know how to react, what I did know was there was a huge branch hurtling towards my face and about to hit

Chapter 13

I sat up in pain and quickly throw myself back to the ground as the memory of the thick branch striking me replayed in my mind in a scarily realistic fashion. I don't know how long I have been out cold for. I have been knocked out a few times in my life, nothing spectacular or amazing stories just clumsiness, the most comical being opening a kitchen cupboard, forgetting I had done it, spinning around, and hitting my head, that knocked me out cold. I also walked past a lady at the gym while she was using a punch bag, admittedly I was too close, and a perfect storm occurred as I bent slightly to tuck my shoelace back into the side of my trainers and she misplaced her hook and cracked me straight on the jaw. Those two were just slight blackouts that could be laughed off. A thick branch to the face hurt, a lot.

I sit up again, the confusion I was feeling slowly dilutes, and clarity begins to form a linear picture board in my brain, my back also hurts, and a quick feel confirms it is covered with scratches, adding the signs of dragging in the ground before me and the fact this is a slightly different area of the woodland, I can deduce that I have been purposefully placed here. Why? I do not know, and I do not know why I am not scared either.

Perhaps intrigue has gotten the best of me or maybe it is the fact that I am somewhere where I do not think I can be found and for the first time in a decade I am 'Nathen-less'. I need to stop thinking about him now, it is an old habit and an unfortunate consequence that once someone is that obsessed with you, you equally become obsessed with them, albeit for very different reasons.

I get to my feet, a little groggy but determined to carry on. A few crows fly off from the branches over me, where they can go, I don't quite know considering how thick the tree's become overhead, it is as if the forest is a self-contained dome. I take a step back and quickly find myself back on my arse as I tumble over a little stone, in fact there is a lot of little stones, and much like myself they appear to have been purposefully placed here.

I decide I need to take a better look at the shape they make so I begin climbing a tree which seemed remarkably accommodating for what I wanted to achieve, I have never climbed a tree before, this seemed very easy. The stones had been arranged to make a symbol, one that I am very sure I had never seen before, yet, it is very familiar, subconsciously I must have seen this before I just can't remember what it means, what does it represent?

I climb back down the tree and kneel by the closest stone, I notice there is something written on each stone, but I do not know what, it isn't in English, there is also some numbers on them and…oh god, these are dates, from and to, these are all gravestones. Okay, now I am scared. I do not know what the arrangement means, I do not know why I have been brought here, I do know I don't like it anymore. I leave that area with haste as a cold goes through my body as if I have dipped into a plunge pool. I want to leave this forest now.

I am completely lost, but I tell myself that is fine because I never really knew where I was anyway. I only have one plan as and it is an obvious one as I find myself utterly out of options, I will just walk, and continue walking until I find myself at the other side, or the way I came in, I know I am on a small island so there is limited capacity to how far this wooded terrain will stretch. Maybe I will bump into my twin, although I would rather not, it is the only possible explanation that it was her that dragged me into a graveyard and left me there unconscious and while that naturally leads to many questions, I am very happy to keep some distance between us, at least until I have calmed down a bit.

I walk fast, simply because it will get me where I am going quicker, but just as I feel like I am making some progress over the ground covered I have a strange feeling which causes a mixture of tunnel vision and vertigo, and it makes it appear like everything ahead of me is stretching out further and my progress is instantly in deficit. From this I can safely say I am not well, maybe the conditions in here mixed with being smacked on the head by what was basically a log has taken its toll. Maybe some of the plants or herbs in here are a hallucinogen and found their way into my system via the various cuts and scratches on my body. Whatever it is it has been a hell of a day and I need to go to bed.

I take a breather and look around trying to determine my next steps and I notice a glow to the right, not too bright, but it is definitely there, and I feel an enticing warmth coming from it and before I had made a conscious decision, I find I am walking in its direction. I feel very ill, and every step is a tremendous strain on my weakening body, but I tell myself that I will be fine once I find the source of the glowing. I do not know why I believe this, but it is enough to keep me going.

I stumble along as the trees twist and morph into laughing faces, thin branches lightly slapping me on my face, the ground heaves up and then down as if it is breathing, and then I hear the ocean, perhaps I am close to getting out, no, I am hearing things, voices now, worried voices, screaming "no, why have you forsaken us, my men, we are doomed, I beg you stop this, why?" and then there is an almighty crash of a wave followed by a snapping noise, I fall to my knees as sea water pours out of my mouth, I cough and splutter, I feel like I am drowning as I hear another deafening crash of waves and screaming. Then in an instance it stops, everything is calm and peaceful, perfectly quiet. I am on my back looking up at the tree's. The fisherman who I seem to see everywhere appears standing over me, holding up a lantern, so that was the source of the glow. I smile, as everything slowly fades to black.

Chapter 14

After losing faith in my male colleagues and the police I became increasingly isolated, I still went to work but I had to constantly change my route so that no two days were the same, or that I didn't do the same pattern on the same day, it all became mentally exhausting. He would sometimes get the same bus as me in the morning, this was unpleasant but not too bad as it was a very busy bus and I made sure I would sit next to somebody, just for that added protection. I stopped going out in the evenings because it started to kill me, just as I was having a good time and beginning to unwind, he would appear, and the claustrophobia would return and the feeling of control over my own life would be taken from me. In a matter of seconds, I could go from being just a relaxed friend and good company, to the main character in someone's else's disturbing story.

The front door to my house was upgraded to having 2 additional locks to the main lock and a chain across the middle. A panic button was fitted by the front door too just in case officer creep decided to 'check in' on me again. Evenings would be a lonely time, at first, I almost enjoyed the change of pace and slowing down, but too much of anything is bad, and I become bored and imprisoned in my own home.

I would have tea while watching TV then have a quick bath, then read a book with a glass of red wine and repeat. Most nights I would spot Nathan walking past my house, and then back again a few minutes later. I was also in the nasty habit of waiting until I got to bed to start worrying about which route, I could take to work the following morning, which usually led to a lot of overthinking and loss of sleep.

It was around this time that Internet chat rooms became my saving grace, it felt a bit corny, and the chat room 'boom' had been and gone 20 years prior, but there were still some support groups out there where people can come together virtually and ease their minds by sharing their problems. After trying a few counselling and therapy groups I decided that the virtual chat arena was for me, but I needed something more direct.

I appreciated every single person that responded to a comment I made, but the variety of issues being addressed at any one time did not help combat the loneliness, and so I began using search engines for 'victims of stalking'. Symbolic of the world we live in this offered up a lot of pornography videos before I the results I actually wanted.

The chatroom changed my life, I was no longer alone, I wanted to stay in and chat to fellow victims and empathise with one and other, none of the others had a similar experience to me when talking to the police which restored some faith in that department, and some of them had experiences that made mine seem tame, sometimes with very violent outcomes. But the purpose of the support group was working perfectly, I would get home from work, make my tea, pour a glass of red, and then open my laptop and begin chatting, sometimes the chats completely strayed from the impact of stalking on daily lives, and I began to feel like I was catching up with friends.

Eventually a group of us exchanged phone numbers and created a group chat so that we could be in constant contact with each other, we were able to give each other live updates 'he's on the same bus as me' 'he keeps jogging past me in the park' 'she's just tried the handle on my car door' we could instantly empathise and advise one another. It made me feel safer, it gave me a bit of my confidence back, and it was inadvertently helping me keep a log of Nathan and his movements around me.

One member of the group began to message me outside of the chat, she wanted to know more about my experience and what my plan was. I was intrigued by the question, I didn't really have a plan, I had hoped it would all go away one day. A plan that was neither pragmatic nor proactive. She then told me a story of her friend who was in a similar situation to mine and how she one day just sold up and emigrated, she relocated to a remote island and now lives a stalker free, and mostly a stress-free life. Initially it sounded a tad theatrical, and I did not believe it would be the resolution for me, I would rather take back what Nathan had taken from me rather than move away and start a fresh.

The thought of moving away and being free kept playing on my mind, I increasingly flirted with the idea until it became a desire of mine. I was in the kitchen one evening waiting for the microwave to ding and confirm my microwave meal for one was ready for consumption, I did generally prefer to cook fresh, but I had felt lazy on this occasion so opened the treasure chest that is the freezer. It began to get a bit 'stuffy' in the kitchen so I went to open the window to let some air in and the window opened about 3 centre metres and jarred, it wouldn't move forwards or backwards, and that minor inconvenience was the inspiration for my big decision, fuck that, I want to leave.

I messaged my friend and said 'okay, I want to disappear and start anew. Could you let your friends know'.

She replied 2 minutes later 'Done'.

Chapter 15

I woke up and instantly felt super warm and cosy, I did not open my eyes as I was hoping I might drift off again. My pillow was large and fluffy and had a sturdiness that meant while I would sink into it, it still supported my neck just right. The duvet was heavy and thick but felt so soft and warm, without opening my eyes I stretched out and did a huge yawn. As I stretched, I felt the aches and bruises on my body, the cuts on my feet and back, the impact of a tree branch hitting my face hard, and had the realisation, how am I now in bed?

I opened my eyes quickly and looked around the room, I was alone, how did I get here? I looked under the duvet half expecting to be chained to the foot of the bed, but I wasn't, I was fully clothed and not restricted in anyway. There is something so familiar about all this, the room, the smell, all of it. I slowly climbed out of the bed and stretched out again, this time I felt every injury from the forest a little more, I walked, with a slight limp, over to the window in the room, judging by the shape of the ceiling I am in a converted roof and the view from the window confirmed I was on an upper floor.

I was surrounded by woodland and trees and so I suspect I am in a house within the woods. It may seem odd to some that there is a house here, but it makes sense to me. I look around the room and it is somehow decorated to my taste. I am not going to question any of this right now. I am just going to enjoy it. It's the first time in a long time I have felt comfortable.

I looked in the wardrobe, out of curiosity rather than necessity and was awestruck with the collection of shoes, boots, shoes, coats, dressing gowns, a real treasure trove of outfits, all things I would buy, all in my size, how? My mind is racing with questions, but I want to ignore the siren going off in my head, I am being looked after and pampered and I won't risk ruining this feeling by overthinking the, admittedly, haunting events I have experienced.

I can rationalise it for the most part by telling myself that this is where I was meant to end up, it explains the perfect wardrobe, it explains the difficulty in getting here, and while a smoother commute would have been desirable, I guess some things are worth a bit of fight, and freedom is very high up on that list.

I stroll down the stairs, I can't seem to stop smiling, I am happy. The stairs are wooden and old-fashioned looking, but they don't creek, they don't even feel harsh on my feet, in fact, every step I take feels padded. This is like luxury living so far, I should have done this sooner. The stairs lead to a small living area, there is no TV but there is a huge bookcase filled end to end with books, so that is fine with me, there's a further view of the woods from the windows, luckily there are good thick curtains too because I imagine it can be rather spooky come night fall. I sit on the cream two-seater sofa and let out a relaxed sigh and stretch my legs out again, I am going to read every single one of those books on this sofa, this is beyond comfortable. A low groan turning into an embarrassing roar was my stomach confirming I was beginning to feel a little peckish, so I decide to further explore my abode.

I strolled over into the kitchen, thinking about omelettes, coffee, yogurt, fruit, bacon, sausages, fresh juice, maybe I am not peckish, I am absolutely starving. The kitchen did not disappoint, it had a little kitchen island, I had always wanted one of them, pure cottage vibes throughout and the fridge, cupboards, and pantry were full to bursting. It would take me an age to even make a dent on this much food. I decide on a tomato, mushroom and spinach omelette, with a freshly ground coffee, and just to really indulge, a pan aux chocolate. Merci beaucoup.

As is human nature my mind began to drift from the short-term marvel to more long-term practicalities. Does someone else live here? Surely, I have not just been gifted a beautiful cottage to live in, will I need to find work once my money runs low? Who replenished this kitchen? If I do need to work, how will I ever find my way out of the woods.

I take a seat and quietly remind myself; this is the good kind of stress and I have time on my side to figure it out, the obviously glaring issues I am trying to ignore are what happened to the other me? I'll call her She-Me, and holy shit how weird is it that that has actually happened, who is the fishman I keep seeing, and finally why did She-Me drag me to a small graveyard and why did, presumably, the fisherman pick me up and carry me to bed? And that is just the tip of the iceberg of weird things that have happened. But I am not bothered, somehow, I genuinely do not care, I feel like I belong here, in my cottage.

The other room downstairs did not offer much really, it was an empty room with the front door out of the cottage, but I liked it was empty, if I am to stay here then there is a room which I could decorate myself and sprinkle my own personality into. Having said that, this cottage does seem to 'get me' it certainly does not need any dramatic changes.

There was another door in the empty room, it looked small but upon closer inspection I could see there were steps leading down to it. Each step towards this door seems to make the temperature drop and I start to get goosebumps on my arms, I try the handle which felt like ice and it is like it shoots a short but sharp electric shock up my arm, it was almost like a warning, but thinking logically I assume this door leads to the cellar, and it is currently locked, which is fine. I will check that out when I am feeling a bit braver.

I go to walk back into the living room torn between if I should have a good look at the bookcase, maybe even sit down on the sofa and indulge in one of them or go back to bed and have a bit more sleep, it had been quite a journey, and I am both physically and mentally exhausted. As I am about to leave the empty room there is a knock on the door. First it was a gentle rap that I only just heard, then as I turned to face the door there were 3 very loud aggressive knocks.

I walked over with natural trepidation, I have a sick feeling that Nathan had found me but try to shake it off, I open the door just a crack and stuck my foot behind it, out of habit more than anything else, but stood on the porch in her cloak was She-Me.

"You" we both say simultaneously.

"Stop that" again in unison.

"Grass crabs and lab rats" we both blurt out in perfect symmetry and then take a step back and smile at each other.

This time she spoke, wincing slightly, "Well, are you going to let me in?".

Chapter 16

I took a step back, she mirrored the action moving forwards, we both said, "right then", I was beginning to hate the mirroring thing, it was curious at first, scary at times, now it is beginning to become frustrating, I have questions, I want to her to tell me everything she knows about me, or is that us? About the Island, is she the person I was sent here to meet, the person that can help?

We walk in perfect symmetry to the kitchen, I can't help but think we would be amazing in a three-legged race, and without speaking, but instinctively, we pull a chair each side of the table and face each other. We both say, "you must have questions". I sigh and drop my head down, feeling defeated, she does the same. "You don't always repeat me, you said things independently before can't you do that now?" we both say. She shook her head; I had an urge to copy but didn't.

We both stood up banging our hands on the table and screaming "talk to me" she then let out a scream as if she was in pain and looking as if she is breaking out of an invisible hindrance. She grabbed a knife off the kitchen side and stabbed it into my leg, not fully, but enough to dig it into the flesh, enough to make it instantly start bleeding, enough to make it hurt like hell. "Why the fuck did you do that?" I took time to acknowledge the pain while she sat down and withdrew her hood and smiled at me, not even blinking, or acknowledging the fact she had just stabbed me, I somewhat poorly reiterated "what the fuck?"

"Oh, will you calm down".

"You stabbed me!"

"Nonsense! Stab is such a violent, nasty word. Stab! I cut you, I cut you cleanly and deep enough to leave a scar".

"Oh, just enough to leave a scar, you cut me just the right amount, that's okay then".

"I know what sarcasm is, you know!"

"Why did you do that?"

"Because now there is a slight difference between us, and I can talk to you freely".

I looked at her in disbelief, "and you couldn't cut your own leg?"

"My dear if you knew the pain it caused me simply breaking free enough to do what I did you would be thanking me for what I have done".

I thought about what she for a second and then to my own surprise said "sorry" I think that, although I did not understand, what she said seemed sincere, I felt there was an element of sacrifice on her part, and she had made that sacrifice for me.

"So, we can have a proper conversation now? Now that we are not…identical copies?"

"Pretty much"

"Jesus, and who has made that a rule? How is this happening? Why are you a copy of me?"

"Oh, but that is arrogant to think is it not?"

"Pardon?"

"How can we ever know who the copy is and who is the original?"

"But my whole life…"

"And you assume, wrongly, that I only came into existence once you appeared on this island".

"…but, okay, yes, I sound a bit arrogant. But I am so confused".

"What would you like to know darling? Perhaps I could help".

"Did you drag me to that burial site in the woods".

"yes"

"Because?"

"You had been knocked out; I knew you would be safe there. Wildlife will not touch the soil in those parts as it is sacred to the island".

"Um, right, okay"

She reaches across the table and slaps me "don't you disrespect us!" she gathers composure and adjusts her outfit accordingly.

I sit in shock and let my mouth work on autopilot "why do you wear a cloak".

She looks down and laughs, she looks beautiful when she does that, wait, gross, stop.

"It is the perfect accessory. It's open and thin which is perfect for the climate here. I can wrap it around myself and lower the hood and it makes a perfect disguise. And honestly, I just love it, I think it suits me."

We both smile, then laugh. She continues. "That reminds me, I did something for you today, something that will begin to get rid of the …shall we call it, pest control problem you have".

This must be the first time in my life that talking about a cloak has reminded someone of something, "Really? Tell me more"

"I stopped by your admirer's accommodation earlier".

"What? Why?"

"Well, it is all part of the plan my dear".

"What plan?"

"To free you of course, to give you the freedom you deserve, the freedom everybody should have".

"Oh, my goodness, thank you so much, thank you. What is this plan? What happened at his accommodation? Did he see you?"

"Slow down, it will become apparent in time, the plan is none of your concern, you're on our Island and we will look after you. He didn't see me, but the most curious thing made me stop in my tracks, he had a travel cot set up, and a pram folded at the side of his room, and inside the cot was a, he had, there was a pumpkin".

"Yeah, that is our baby" I noted her perfectly justifiable puzzled response and quickly caught myself, "sorry, yes, it is a pumpkin, he thinks, and this is the level of crazy we are dealing with, he thinks that pumpkin is our baby". This is something that always used to freak me out and made me feel sick, but being here, with help and support and saying it out loud, I actually found it to be quite funny.

"He think's a pumpkin is your baby? He thinks it's real? I heard him trying to kick the door down before I left the room, like he was trying to break in and get his child, how delightful…"

She then burst out laughing, and hearing the idiocy, I too began to laugh, and we laughed together as Nathans hold over me turned from scary to ridiculous. My laughter turned to a slight giggle and faded down, ended with a sort of gentle joyful sigh. Her laughter continued, it got louder and more intense, she began to frighten me, leaning over the table laughing in my face hysterically. The sound of her laughter transformed slightly as if the audio was being possessed by something demonic. She suddenly froze, still leaning over the table, she was still in my face, and she was still smiling, laughing even, but without the sound.

"Are you oka…"

She burst into life interrupting my question and began punching the table with her hand shouting "She-Me, that's what you call me, She-Me, that's what you call me, SHE-ME, THAT'S WHAT YOU FUCKING CALL ME, SHE-ME, SHE-ME" she got so loud that I had to cover my ears. I started to squint my eyes to protect me from what I could see before me, but I needed to keep them open enough to remain alert. And as quick as it started it stopped.

She sat down adjusted her outfit and cleared her throat.

"Are you okay?"

"Yes, my dear"

"What just happened?"

"I don't know what you mean?"

"We were just talking about the pumpkin and…"

"Yes, the pumpkin baby" she scoffed, "how utterly tragic but tremendously funny".

"Are you okay?"

"Yes, you keep asking me that? Are you okay?"

We sat and looked at each other, it was obvious to me that she was not willing to discuss what had just happened, or even that she knew it had happened. But I am not going to push this now. She stood up slowly and began to untie her cloak, she spoke while doing so, "you need to be at the lighthouse tomorrow night at 11pm by the way, that way you'll see our plan come to fruition".

"I don't know how to get there?"

"Well, set of early then my dear, and figure it out. I am leaving this cloak here; it is very important you wear this if you leave the house. Be sure to blend in".

"Will you be okay without it? Would you like a jacket?"

She laughed, and thankfully stopped short of going into the manic laughter again. "Are you going to walk me to the door?"

I walked her to the door, of course, she turned to me and said "try not to think too much, just rest now, enjoy the solitude of being here" I nodded in agreement. She lifted my chin with her finger and kissed me on the lips, I had wanted to kiss her for ages, and I know that's incredibly narcissistic, but it is the truth, I closed my eyes willing myself to melt further into the kiss, but the sensation had gone, and when I opened my eyes, she was gone. I cannot believe that just happened. Now that she is gone it didn't feel like it was right, but it definitely did feel right at the time, my heart is still racing a bit.

I look down at my leg where she had stabbed me and there was a generous amount of blood around the wound, I will need to wash these jeans. However, this has given me the perfect excuse to go and have a long bath.

Chapter 17

If I recall correctly, I was sent a package about three days after I had confirmed to my friend, I was ready to start a new life. It was a pleasant surprise and one that really engulfed the burning desire to move. The package contained a travel agents' brochure which gave me a bit of background and popular spots on the island.

It also contained a SIM card with a sticky label attached that read 'only use once you are on the boat' okay, noted, no pun intended. The package also gifted me some old-fashioned looking books, I flicked through one of them, but it was all written in foreign language and I did not speak anything other than English. In fact, I didn't speak anything other than Yorkshire, and I think that's alrate.

One of the books was leather bound with a nice cotton bookmark, very posh looking. It had a symbol on the front which I did not recognise but it definitely added to the intrigue, I had a quick flick through the pages and while it was all written in foreign, it felt special, it felt important, and I noticed that it was entirely handwritten which to me added to the privilege of possessing such.

Continuing what seemed to be a never-ending streak of calamity, while flicking through these incredibly thin pages I got a paper cut, this didn't even seem possible, other than its me and this kind of stuff happens to me. My blood dripped down a page of this handwritten relic, a book that looks like it is a few hundred years old and has been treasured, and it now has a stain on it after being in my possession for less than four minutes. I pick it up and put it back in the package, leaving bloody prints on everything I touch.

I washed my thumb in the kitchen and put a plaster on it as it gushed an excessive amount for such a small cut, I always hated how much paper cuts sting. I went and placed the package on the sofa so I could have another look after work and left the house with a renewed spring in my step. That day was the day I handed in my one months working notice.

I went to the staff canteen for my lunch and had a coffee and chocolate brownie, I rang my friend to tell her I had received a package.

"I got a package from, erm…the island people? Your friends"

"Oh lovely, I wouldn't really class them as friends. But this is wonderful news".

"That sounded harsh, do you not like them?"

"I don't really know them to be honest, I know bits, I have heard bits, but I worked for them for a couple of years".

"Nice, doing what?"

"It is complicated to explain, for the sake of a title though we'll say recruitment".

"Were they a good employer?"

"They helped people that needed help".

"Well, that's me. The package had, what looked like a really old handwritten book inside it"

The phone fell silent, I pulled it from my ear to make sure we hadn't been disconnected. The timer was still ticking by, I spoke again "are you still there?"

There was a bit more silence before she responded, "I'm here".

"Oh, I thought we'd been cut off, so yeah, I was saying there was this really old book…"

"I heard you".

"Erm, right, well I was going to say I feel bad because I cut my thumb and got blood on the pages".

There was more silence, again, causing me to look at my phone, without wanting to sound needy I asked again "are you still there?" there was a loud sniff, as if she had been crying, or had a cold, before she spoke "it is nice they sent you that, they must like you".

I was about to ask her what she had told them about me, but she essentially ended the call, "look I must go, just promise me one thing…please just, just be careful yeah. I hope this all works out for you, I really do, I just hope the cost isn't too great. I'm sorr…"

That time we were cut off; I am certain she hung up. She sounded happy, overwhelmed and then I sensed some trepidation in her voice, I began to consider if I had rushed into this and if I had made the right choice. Sure, I had just handed my notice in, but I am very good at analysis, I'll get another job if I decide to stay in Sheffield. I just felt confused by my friend telling me to be careful. The same friend who encouraged me to leave.

I travelled home that night considering all my options and deciding that I would have a glass of red and read through the holiday brochure and see if that reignites my certainty to leave. I did notice that I hadn't seen Nathan for a couple of days, what if he has lost interest in me? I would be moving for nothing. Maybe he has just gotten better at hiding. That idea creeped me out and as soon as I got home, I double checked every door, window, and cupboard in my house. I confess, I also had a quick look in the washing machine and spoiler, he wasn't hiding in there. Considering everything, he has either moved on and potentially stalking someone else, has improved at stalking and I haven't detected him, or he is planning something. And while I have questions like this that I don't know the answer to I decided to commit and move.

I entered my living room that night and gasped, before I had gone to work, I left the parcel on my sofa, now the contents had been spilt over my floor and the parcel itself had been torn down the middle. I frantically ran around my house looking in each room, nothing else had been disturbed, nothing had been touched or taken, but someone had been in my house and had done this deliberately, but I do not know who, why, or what message they are trying to send?

Chapter 18

During times as these I had to try and think objectively and not let Nathan be the only cause of problems. While I like to think positively, dangers are all around, so while my instant thought was that Nathan had broken into my house and ripped my parcel up and scattered the contents on the floor, I cannot afford to put the blame on him and assume it is case closed.

Another, more thorough search of my home concluded that there was no forced entry anywhere, again, nothing had been taken or disturbed. This made no sense, there was no logic to why this had happened or what the motivation may have been. For obvious reasons I decided to not inform the police, so I had a decision to make, I could brush it off and salvage what was left of the evening, or I could let it eat away at me until I hid under my duvet and passed out with all the lights on. I chose the former.

I read through the brochure, and I loved what I was reading, the adjectives peaceful and escapism were used throughout and really captivated me. I passed on drinking wine that evening because I intended to remain alert, and I wanted to make sound decisions.

There was not much further reading on the internet about Melas, and this did strike me as odd, however, there was an article about a great shipwreck from a couple of hundred years ago which was a haunting read, many fishermen lost their lives in an unprecedented storm. It is a tragedy that still casts gloom upon on the island. Selfishly, I can live with the horrible history, rather than a party island, respectfully.

Naturally I knew how my mind worked so I needed to be proactive further still, and so I emailed an estate agent to arrange a free valuation of my property. I made clear my intention was to leave it open as a 'to rent, ready furnished'. That way I don't have to rehouse, sell, or store my things, and going through an estate agent means they can play at landlord, albeit for more than fair cut of the monthly rent, I'm sure.

I went to bed feeling good, I had made a lot of brave first steps and set off wheels in motion. My friends on the island would send me travel details and tickets which was a tremendous gesture and one I hope was an accurate reflection of their character. I try desperately to remain positive about all this, but in the back of my mind I was aware that being at the mercy of strangers and relying on their kindness or good intention was slightly naive to say the least. But desperate times.

I woke up feeling the freedom that comes with handing in your notice at a job, for the next four weeks I will be looking busy, promising handover notes I will never write and showing a determination to stay focused, but the real commitment is to the façade I will portray. The feel-good factor quickly turned to confusion as I looked to my bedside table and noticed the leather-bound book was sat there, open on the page that had blood on it. I remember clearly putting this on my bookcase last night so how did it get here? Who placed it there?

I tiptoed out of bed, not wishing to make a noise in case it alerted a potential intruder, but once I reached my door the bravery drained from me and what I thought was adrenaline was fear and I coward by my door shaking all over. I said in a whisper "please just leave me alone" I sunk my head into my knees before a thud woke me from my turmoil.

I looked up and saw the book had fell off the bedside table, I stood up and walked over to see if I could feel a draft of some sort. I stopped dead and screamed as I caught a glance of my reflection in my dressing table mirror. It was me, but I looked old, there was a wound across my forehead with maggots eating into my skull, my jaw hung as if it had been broken and my skin looked wrinkled and grey. Another thud interrupted my scream as a bird fly into my bedroom window.

I looked at the oily outline left by the bird, I caught a glimpse of it on the patio below, snapped neck, dead. Next doors cat was already sizing it up. I instantly looked back to the mirror, I am me again, normal me. What the hell happened. I went for a shower and questioned what seemed to be an obvious deteriorating mental state, I could not shake the image of my reflection, the grey rotting reflection, and I actively avoided mirrors from then because I was scared.

I went downstairs to make a coffee and have a bowl of Greek yoghurt and honey. I went into the living room to grab my handbag and body mist before leaving for work and noticed the old book was on the bookshelf where I had left it. I could not believe it, I ran back upstairs to my bedroom and looked to the floor where it had been, it wasn't there. How is this book moving around my house and who would inflict such mental torture on me? Thank God I am leaving this house!

Inside my little cloakroom under the stairs there was a sliding door cupboard on the floor, I had never had a purpose for it before now. But I grabbed all the books that had been sent to me, including the one that seemed to follow me, and stored them in there. Out of sight out of mind. I made a promise to myself that If I got home from work that evening and the books had moved from that spot, which would mean going through two closed doors, I would walk straight back out and sleep at my parents.

Chapter 19

I stood in the mirror wearing She-Me's' cloak, I don't think I look super-hot or anything in this, what is it about her that is so alluring? I untie the cloak and take a dressing gown out of the wardrobe. If there is one command, I am able to comply with right now it is get comfortable and relax. I climbed into the bed, surprised that it was somehow more snuggly than I remember it being and I begin to thumb through a book, I am really excited as is the new one by my favourite author, which I hadn't had the opportunity to buy, such was the hectic nature of the city centre rat race. I move here, look at the bookcase and there it is, sitting there proud, almost presenting itself to me, and it has been signed.

There must be a book shop somewhere on this island as I can't imagine online purchases finding their way to this cottage. I look at the clock to my right on the bedside table. I have quite a few hours before I need to be at the lighthouse. I decide to chill out for an hour or two before trying to navigate my way through these woods and back to the island centre and hopefully somewhere lighthouse adjacent.

I wake up with a start and instantly look towards my bedside to check the time, I had been asleep for an hour and 25 minutes, I relaxed in the knowledge that I had not overslept. The startled awakening dissolved into what I can accept was standard behaviour of being cosy, warm, reading and subsequently falling asleep, although I stress that is not a reflection of the literature.

I get dressed and go downstairs, picking up my cloak on route, I eat a banana quickly and have a glass of water and go to leave the cottage. Going into the entrance room I find a key hung up by the door which comes as a relief as I was beginning to wonder how and if I should lock the door when I leave. I am still unsure if this is now my place, or if I share it with someone I haven't met yet.

Just as I take the key from the wall, I hear a thud, quickly followed by two more dull sounds, I look across the room and it is coming from, what I assume, is the cellar door. What the hell. I walk over to the door as the nocking continues, the power of the knock seems to be building as does the frequency of the sound. "Hello? Hello? Is somebody there? Are you trying to get in…or out maybe?" . The knocking stops as I get closer, I try the handle again and it remains locked.

I am about to walk away when an almighty crash against the door happens, causing me to fall backwards, the door remains intact but there is definitely someone trying to get in. "Hello?" I shout again, knowing I probably will not get a response. What if this key is for this door I ponder, I slowly enter the key into the lock, unsure if I am doing the right thing or not, the key begins to turn and then hits resistance, I was somewhat relieved that this wasn't the right key and I hastily leave the cottage and lock the front door, just as the banging on the door begins again.

I walk down the cute path from the cottage to what looks like a crossroads in this absolute jungle woodland. I look up and see that the trees have knitted together some of their branches to create 'the symbol' the same one I saw when I woke up after being knocked out on my way here. I took a few steps and then looked up at it again and gasp as I have the realisation that it is the same symbol that was on the cover of the old leather book I was sent. I knew it looked familiar, I just couldn't place it, but of course that is where I know it from. I feel a sense of relief knowing that where I am and what is happening is all part of the plan, and my obsession to be free is shared by others.

I pull the hood up on my cloak and begin to look around the woods to determine if there is an obvious route out of here. I see a flame flicker in the distance, possibly from an oil lantern, maybe a firefly, I can't confirm from this far away, but I instinctively know that I should go towards it, like a moth, no thought, just instinct. Should it be wrong, well, I don't have a better idea. Let's go.

Chapter 20

I come out the other side of the woods which I was relieved was a lot less eventful than when I first entered them. The flickering flame seems no closer to me than it was when I first noticed it, but I continue my pursuit. And coming over a little hill which exposed the ocean, albeit in a cascade of darkness, I see a tremendous silhouette of a lighthouse in line with the guiding flame. I either have great instincts or dumb luck, but either way I am not complaining.

Arriving at the lighthouse I see the source of the flame and my first thought was correct, it was an oil lamp held high by the mysterious fisherman, "Hello" I say, knowing that there is a very low chance he will actually respond, but manners cost nothing. I look up at the tall edifice and wonder if I need to wait here with Mr. chatter box or if I should go inside the lighthouse, personally I hope it is the latter because I have never been inside a lighthouse before.

Some hands cover my eyes from behind which initially makes me jump before I relax into it, knowing who it is "guess who?"

"I know who that is".

"It's me, She-Me".

"You don't have to call yourself that".

"You picked the name my dear".

"I don't recall ever saying it out loud", she just stood and smiled at me.

"Anyway, quickly, if you look over there you'll see 'stalky pants' making his way to the lighthouse, so you two need to hurry on up and get inside. I will lock the door behind you and then hide until the time is right".

Any questions I had were outweighed by the sense of urgency and the panic that seeing Nathan evoked within. The fisherman and I were almost bundled into the lighthouse and cast into a deep darkness as we heard the door shut and then lock, the fisherman's lamp offered only a little relief from the pitch black, not enough to light up the surroundings. She-Me whispered through the door "you must hurry to the top, the lock on this door is faulty and doesn't always hold. Oh, and look after my cloak".

"Why? Where are you going? What is your plan?"

"You will see, now hurry my dear, I have to go hide. Goodbye"

I followed the fishman to the spiral staircase, it was either that or stand alone and confused in pitch darkness. I felt this climb up the stairs will have an impact on my knees and thighs, and I am happy I have the super comfortable bed back at the cottage as I will certainly need it tomorrow morning. So many stairs!

Once I got to the top of the lighthouse and regulated my breathing, I took in as much detail as possible. I may have moved here but for now I am a tourist and I have never seen a room like this. "So, this is what the inside of a lighthouse looks like, I wonder where the keeper plugs in the kettle" I say to the fisherman, determined to get a response or reaction out of him eventually, all the while knowing it is futile.

We stand close together looking down at the grounds, I wrap my cloak around me tighter and keep the hood up as it is so very cold in this building, and especially so when my company is close by. I see Nathan pacing around the grounds, there is a familiarity in his movement, he is looking for something. I wonder how they lured him here.

Nathan turns around and seems to almost go rigid before turning soft and open, a quick scan across reveals he is stood opposite She-Me. I really need to stop calling her that. He seems to be talking to her and she is not saying anything, I wish I could hear what was being said. His body language, it looks like he's pleading with her. She is now running towards him, and he has his arms wide open to embrace her. What the hell is this? What are they doing? Wait, she has ran past him, and now he's chasing her, desperately, why? Shit, "the cliff top" I bang on the window "stop her quick, she's going to fall off the cliff" I turn towards the fisherman and somewhat unfairly scream "DO SOMETHING, STOP HER". She-Me gleefully leaps towards the edge of the cliff and spanned out her arms like a diver, Nathan must have missed her by centre meters, and she fell off the cliff top.

"No! no, no, no, she must be, she can't have survived…why the fuck would she do that? D-did she sacrifice herself for me? No, fuck, FUCK! What the fuck". My mind began racing, I recalled what my fiend said on the phone when she first secured me a place on this Island, something about the cost being great, is this what she meant? Just then I noticed Nathan looking up at me and the fisherman and he suddenly ran to the door, of course the lock didn't hold, and I assume he'll be up here within a couple of minutes. He is going to be surprised to see my face. God this is so fucked up.

I could hear Nathans footsteps stampeding below, he seemed angry, or perhaps understandably emotional…I guess. The sound of his steps was dwarfed by the thumping of my heart as my panic caused the decibels of blood flow to create an in-ear drumbeat. I looked in front of me frantically, I inspected the hatch, there was no way out. I looked towards the fisherman, and he was gone. How? how is this happening? I spoke in a loud whisper "where are you? Why did you go?"

A windowpane opens slightly, and the fisherman stook out his hand, not waving, not inviting, but letting me know he was there. Genuis, that particular part of the window mirrored the rest of the room concealing the fact it is a, well I don't know, a panic room, I guess. I climbed inside and sat cross-legged next to the fisherman, I turned and smiled at him, more at the awkwardness of the close quarters I found myself in with him. He barely acknowledged me.

Chapter 21

Nathan eventually entered the room, he looked like he had lost his mind, and he seemed to be dangerous, raging, screaming, shouting, crying, swinging at the air. I hugged my knees and held my breath. The fisherman was stood looking out to sea with his back to all the 'action'.

I was frightened that if we were here long enough that he would eventually figure out we are in this hidden compartment. Like so many times before I just wish he would go away. This time he looked different, he looked deranged. I am not sure how much fight the fisherman has in him if Nathan did discover us, or if he would even get involved.

I felt a tinge of relief as I heard more footsteps running up the stairs, I wondered who it could be? Is it She-Me? Was it all a hoax and now she is coming to save me again from Nathan? That thought was diminished when the sound of footsteps multiplied, and it began to sound like a giant and rampant millipede had taken to the stairs.

Clarity burst through the hatch in the form of police officers who wasted no time in punching Nathan and knocking him unconscious. They proceeded to peel him off the floor and take him down the stairs. It was a very clean punch; I flinched a little when I saw the connection. The last policeman turned to go down the hatch and looked directly where the fisherman and I were hidden, it felt like he knew we were there, he said "we'll get him back to his bed". He then placed a gun on the side and said "just in case somebody may need it" then slammed the hatch shut. He could have been saying that to the other policemen, he most likely was, but it was pretty unnerving how he looked directly at me as he spoke. Who am I kidding, that was definitely directed at me, and it is not even the strangest thing that has happened tonight.

I stood up and stretched, that was a lot of drama to unpack while sitting cross legged and holding my breath. The Fisherman was still stood with his back to room, looking outwards to the ocean. I looked at him and could see his lower lip was quivering and a tear was rolling down his cheek. I had always been open minded about things and the evidence is stacking up to the situation I am facing "you're a ghost aren't you" there was a pause, he did not react. I wasn't really expecting a response, I assume if he was amongst the living, he would have said something to that.

He remained in place staring out to the ocean, another tear rolled down his cheek. So, it turns out ghosts are real, and they do exist. I have the tendency to get a bit goofy when I feel uncomfortable and the croak escaping my throat was an early warning of the verbal diarrhoea that was coming fast, "is there a difference between ghosts and spirits?" "How come you guided me here? Did you used to work at the lighthouse?" "Oh! Can you walk through walls?" I reign myself in, remember he was crying and that I should be more empathic, regardless of which realm he exists within.

Another realisation hits me as I try to determine what he is looking at in the sea, "oh my god, shit, oh I'm sorry, it was your boat wasn't it? It was your boat that is the legend of this island. I'm so, so sorry. You must miss your friends; you must have suffered. I feel awful". He looked at me and this time I saw tears were streaming down both cheeks, "what happened?".

At that moment, as in the woods before, the sound of waves crashed in my ears, cracking wood and the screams of men filled my head, so loud I felt I was experiencing the tragedy, it was as if I was there. Thunder roared as rain relentlessly pummelled the deck and harsh coldness shot down my back. I felt cold and wet, like I would never be dry again, I felt a desperate, helpless need to return home, a snapping noise told me that would never be possible, the ship is sinking. I hear the men cursing at the captain "you did this, you dammed us all, you cursed us! Beg now!! BEG FOR FORGIVENESS, may God have mercy on our soul's you bastard". I gasped for air and fell against the window of the lighthouse, coughing up sea water before blacking out.

The sound of a gentle tide welcomes me back to consciousness, I am warm, I am dry, and I am ridiculously comfortable. I never want this feeling to end, and I keep my eyes closed as opening them would take me away from this dream like state. I'm back in the cottage and in my bed, I don't need to open my eyes to know that there has never been a comfort close to this.

The ocean noise has completely faded, and I find I have transitioned from a harsh sea to a sea of tranquillity. I have to open my eyes as I hear thudded footsteps and I quickly sit up in bed, "She-Me?" of course it isn't, the sadness of watching her jump replays in my head and I feel shame for the comfort I was momentarily enjoying. It was the fisherman, or at least, his ghost, walking to leave my bedroom.

"Thank you!"

He stops in his tracks.

"Thank you for bringing me back safely" He nods without turning around and facing me, he then lets out a sigh and continues to the door.

"I really am sorry for what you went through, truly I am", at this he stops and faces me, saying nothing, doing nothing, but there is an overwhelming sadness in his eyes, and I feel like we connect on some level.

"How come you never speak?"

At this he turned away again and continued his exit, I laid backdown exhausted while trying not to exhibit any self-pity when he turned in the doorway, he then opened his mouth, very wide actually. I recoiled and felt sick but quickly tried to counterbalance that reaction by giving him an empathic look. His tongue had been removed; the remaining jagged wound leads me to believe it was cut off in an unceremonious fashion. Before I could say anything, he turned around again and walked off down the stairs. I laid back down in bed. What am Involved in?!

She-Me, I can't believe it, oh and I am friends with a ghost now. Well, I say friend, does he like me, or is he instructed to watch over me? Oh my god, by who? This is crazy. Nathan might not be a problem anymore, he caught a hell of a punch on the jaw which I have to admit was satisfying to see, and he thinks I am dead now. She-Me, it keeps coming back to her. I look under the duvet and see I am still wearing her cloak and I wrap myself up in it, pulling the hood over my head. I rub the sore on my leg where she stabbed me as it is strange comfort for me now. Never thought I would be having thoughts like this. My head is humming from all the information I am slowly comprehending. I need some more sleep.

Chapter 22

I had places where I felt safe, where I knew Nathan would not be so crazy as to follow me entirely, in my work building for example, once I got into the building and especially up to my floor and my desk, I sensed I could relax a little. A big part of that was that you required a staff badge to move around. He did sometimes show up to feed the birds, but even a stalker finds it difficult to maintain that for 9 hours, boredom aside it would require a lot of breadcrumbs to commit to a full day of bird feeding.

My parents house, that always seemed a safe space, I noticed him walk past the house a few times, but he never lingered, I assume he knew my father would break him if he got his hands on him.

My own home, he had violated the garden and that was slowly becoming a neglected jungle where nature had taken back its rightful place on earth, I did consider hiring a Gardner, but it was fairly expensive, and I liked to think that one day I would be brave enough to go back out there and cut the grass.

The image of where he was once stood staring towards my house still haunts me. Despite him walking past my home in the evenings, I never really felt uncomfortable, it was frustrating, but I had a routine of locking and double checking all the doors and windows as soon as I got in, and from therein I felt safe, and it was my commutes that posed a threat. That changed.

As is so often the case, and at the risk of victim shaming myself, my big 'mistake' was letting my guard down slightly, and daring to think I could have some fun. I had been at work all week and hadn't been followed, my house hadn't been strolled by, and to my knowledge, the garden had not been disturbed. It was so overgrown that it would either make it obvious someone had been there or conceal the fact. As to not psychologically torture myself I stopped trying to guess where he might be, had he lost interest? am I free? and rather turned my attention to being sensible and enjoy it while it lasts.

So, me and my gal pal went for drinks on Eccy road after work, I hate 'gal pal' I do not know why I thought that was suitable, more colleague turning into real life friend if anyone under the age of 30 knows a more hip way of describing such. Her name's Anna and she's an intern at our place but we have really hit it off, she radiates a lot of positive energy which is good for me and she has just got a new boyfriend so she is a super emitter of good vibes, he's called Ed, or Edward…I think, apparently he is some kind of former child prodigy now super genius, Anna says he's a 'fun nerd'. Having not been stalked all week I decided that drinks after work would be fun, and I would treat myself.

I had more pints than I should have done, but it had been the first time in ages I had relaxed and enjoyed socialising with someone. I did not get ridiculously drunk, but I am certain I was somewhere between tipsy and drunk, between the shadows and the real. I got a taxi home, it was my preferred method of nighttime transport and later stumbled down my driveway, I rummaged through my handbag and became entangled in my lanyard, before dropping my perfume on the floor, it sounded like it smashed but it was pretty much finished anyway. I managed to scrape the key into the lock on my third or fourth attempt and hopped inside while removing my footwear. The alcohol had slightly compromised my centre of gravity and I propped myself up against my hallway wall. I then noticed rose petals sprinkled across my floor, I instantly felt sick, I felt violated, I knew straight away, he was in my home.

I looked up and there he was, stood there smiling and said, "Surprise".

My body reacted to the situation faster than my thought process and I began shaking and looking around confused, how did he get in here? I had to say something.

"Nathen I…Nathen…what the fuck? You've broken into my home".

"Well, you've made that sound a bit sinister, how else can I set up a surprise for you?"

"How did you get in here?" he looked towards the kitchen window, that bloody window.

"I came in through the window".

"You broke into my home".

"I entered through the window".

"Can you hear yourself? Get the fuck out"!

I glanced around and noticed he had written his name across my mirror with my lipstick, and he had pinned uploads of photos of me that he had taken without me knowing, an archive of his stalking habits.

"Sylvia let's just calm down okay. This is a nice surprise".

"That is not your decision to make".

I noticed my closet door was open, I quickly pushed past him, the sliding component was open, the book I hidden in there was gone.

"Why have you been in here? Where's my book?"

"Ah yeah, that book, looked really cool but I couldn't understand a word it said" and he let out a chuckle like we were friends.

"Don't you dare laugh at that book, it needed to stay in there, where did you put it?"

"Calm down, it's here in the kitchen…wait, no it was right there, right before you came in…where is it?"

"…Nathan get the fuck out before I call the police"

"Sylvia wait, just quickly"

"What?"

He produced an engagement ring and said to me with emotion in his voice and big puppy dog eyes "I love you will you marry me".

"Fuck you"

"Sylvia, we're soulmates, we will always be together. I would follow you to the ends of the earth, to the moon and back, we may as well make it official…right?"

"There is no such thing as soulmate's you twerp, now please fuck off, take that fucking ring with you, and don't you dare try some shit like this again".

He then pushed me against the wall, his eyes widened, and he looked wild, like he had lost all sense of self. "YOU BELONG TO ME! SAY YES. MAKE IT OFFICIAL, YOU ARE MINE".

Nathen quickly stepped back knowing he had crossed the line yet again, that he could have hurt me, and in this instance, I knew I would never get rid of him, he was right, I belonged to him and there is no getting away from him. I looked down and started to cry, I was scared, alone, and could not form any words of protest. He walked past me grabbed my wrist and forced the engagement ring onto my finger and said, "I'll set a date" he then got to the doorway and said, "Love you. Now, make sure you lock the door behind me, there could be a lunatic out there".

Remarkable how quickly such an interaction can sober you up.

Chapter 23

I strolled through to the kitchen, I could see my little bonsai tree had been a victim of the break in, and my mug. But where is that book? It was apparent he had filled dishwasher, but my thinking was that I would bin every small possession I have now knowing he's been in my house.

The window looked slightly more ajar than it did before, I make the decision for calling out a 24/7 emergency window repair tradesman and curse myself for not doing it sooner. Having decided to move away I became very prudent about any expenditure on the house. A stupid mistake.

I realised I was still wearing the engagement ring on my finger and quickly pulled it off, taking a chunk of my knuckle with it, I did not feel the pain if there was any, I pulled open the front door so hard it bounced back after the slamming the wall, I put my hand out to catch it and then threw the ring out into the street to put as much distance between me and it as was possible and then screamed some profanity.

Unfortunately, an elderly man was walking past, enjoying his evening stroll, however he suddenly stopped in his tracks to look at me, in shock, on my knees and crying. He looked like he was about to ask me something, probably ask if I'm okay, but then he thought better of it and continued walking. His gentle evening stroll turned to walk with haste and do not look back, like I was Eurydice.

The window was repaired quickly, I think I had made the tradesman uncomfortable as I was clearly shaken and had been crying. This meant he did not want to stay a second longer than necessary and also gave me a mate's rates 20% off. I checked around my house and thankfully the rooms upstairs did not appear to have been violated, and my underwear drawer was undisturbed, so that was a relief. I think I would have been sick had he gone through there.

I sat in the living room with a cup of tea, there was the option of some biscuits to dip of course, but I was not in the mood. I was just staring at the screen, I couldn't tell you what I was watching, I was too far gone in my own mind. I began thinking about my new life on the Island and how wonderful it could prove to be, equally I was unnerved about how Nathan said he would follow me anywhere, as if he knew what I was planning. There had been stuff around the house alluding it, but I did not know how long he was here or how thorough he was. It was horrible I was even having to consider such things.

I was so relieved the next day was the start of the weekend because this evening, despite starting so well with drinks with Anna, has been a terrible ordeal. Looking on the bright side the window in the kitchen had been fixed at least. I closed my eyes and rolled my head back to the headrest of the chair, the pain it shot down my spine told me that I must be pretty tense. Understandably so if I do say so myself.

Just as I was beginning to drift off, I was woken by a thump on my nose and shot up in my chair. It was reminiscent of when I fall asleep in bed while reading and the book gives me a punch for having the audacity to fall asleep while reading. To further add to the confusion it was a book, the book in fact, where the hell did that come from. I picked it up and flicked through it again. What does this stuff mean? There was some of my hair caught on the pages, I did not want to consider where it had dropped from because there was no logical explanation. I got to the page where I had received a papercut a few weeks ago and screamed slamming the book shut again. My blood from the cut it gave me was still wet, it was still seeping into the spine of the book like it was relaying on a loop, how was that possible? It isn't possible. What the fuck?!

I threw the book back into the hidden compartment of the closet space and said "stay in there you weird little bastard" then tried to block it from my mind. If I had attempted to comprehend the events of that evening I would have, almost certainly, cracked up.

And with that, it is bedtime.

Chapter 24

I awoke in my little cottage. My first thoughts were of She-Me, and then of the Fisherman's cut off tongue, or at least what was left of it. I couldn't help but acknowledge how comfortable I was in this bed, despite the horror preoccupying my mind. A few more minutes won't hurt.

I awoke in my little cottage. This bed is bad for me. I have never experienced such perfect comfort. Such warmth and protection. Like a baby in the womb...

I awoke in my little cottage. I do not even remember falling to sleep that time. I sat up quickly to avoid falling back to sleep. The clock informed me that I was well into the afternoon. Assuming it was the same day. I would not be surprised if I had managed to sleep through a whole day and I am now halfway through the following day. I can't even think of how I would know. Being 'off the grid' is trippy. Maybe I should sleep on the sofa tonight, I don't want to start my new life being a lazy arse.

Stretching was definitely a luxury I could now afford. In my past life, well not past life, my stalked/working life I would wake up, acknowledge I was tired, acknowledge I ached all over then I would yawn and stretch quickly and start getting ready for work. Now I feel like I am doing 30 minutes of yoga under my duvet. Allowing myself another good long stretch I felt a sudden jolt. I looked around questioning what it could have been but nothing obvious had disturbed the room. I got back into my stretching when I felt another harsh nudge and a thud. The thud came from beneath the bed.

I quickly jumped out of the bed to see if it happened again, and I caught sight of some fingertips just behind the far bed post. The hand quickly disappeared as I yelped and then gasped, catching the yelp in a big breath, and forcing it back into my mouth with my hands. The bed began to shake vigorously causing ornaments in the room to vibrate towards the edge of their respective shelves like an old mobile phone on silent mode. The bed stopped shaking and the room fell silent, it was quiet before but now it was like I'd lost my hearing.

I crouched down, quivering like a defecating canine, scared of what I might see. I looked towards the back of the bed where I first saw the hand, nothing there. I scanned across the length of the bed and there was nothing there. What the hell is happening? I then heard a shuffling noise and looked straight back towards the end of the bed where I had first checked and there was a pair of eyes starring right back at me, I screamed, the person shuffled away from under the bed.

I looked up, away from the floor and over the mattress to face the incongruity in my bedroom, but there was no one there. Just as I was about to try and rationalise what was happening, two bloody hands shot out from under the bed and grabbed my ankles and with ease pulled me under the bed, I did not even have time to scream it happened that fast.

Suddenly I was on the floor under my bed being mounted by an unknown force, none of this seemed physically possible, its speed and strength, the way it is on top of me, there is not enough room under the bed for this. It moved from my legs and crawled up me until it was face to face with me. And as soon as we were face to face, I recognised it, recognised her, "She-Me, but you…I saw you…how?" but she did not answer she morphed in front of me, she became the very image I saw of myself before in the mirror, before I moved to this island, she was me, but dead, rotting, her mouth was secreting a tar across my chest and neck.

I was struggling and screaming for her to get off me. She began convulsing and shaking, and she began rotting quickly, the smell was so bad and so intense that I could taste it, I could feel it as I breathed in, I could feel it leaving my skin pores. She-Me began shaking and making an animalistic noise, a snort, a growl, and then she burst into thousands of maggots. I could not stop it; I swallowed so many of them. They were in my ears, in my tear ducts, everywhere. I rolled around under the bed, hoping to squash and kill as many of them as possible.

I span onto my front, and crawled away from underneath the bed, coughing profusely and spitting out maggots on the floor. I was not in pain, but I could feel the maggots on me, inside me and I wanted to peel off my skin and squash them all. But I couldn't, all I did was pass out.

I awoke on my floor. Did not stretch or feel tired. Just free. Finally, I understand who I am. I know my purpose. He is close I can sense it. I am not scared. Let him come.

Chapter 25

My life story could have been so different, I could have been the bad guy, the villain, or if people were being kind – the victim that snapped. Through all the bullshit with Nathan, all the stalking, breaking into my house, all of it, there was a time where I wanted to kill him, I became that desperate, so hurt, so angry. Nonetheless, had I done that, I would have been brought before a court and I would have been tried as a murderer, alas, a murderer with a sob story.

My bond with my dad was a special. He was a tough as nails Yorkshireman, but he loved his kids dearly. He may have worked in the Steel works his whole life, he may have had a tattoo up his arm that read 'Sheffield' but that was visible as he hugged me and my brothers. My brothers had a different relationship with him than I did, theirs was a love based on respect. Mine was a love because I was his little girl, the princess of the family and I grew up having the perks of such.

The bond with my Mum was healthy, I loved her, she loved me, but there wasn't a sense that I was the centre of her universe. We would enjoy the cliché shopping trips, salons, cinema dates and other things which I guess would make us 'basic bitches' and proud of it. However, she would occasionally make digs at me, nothing too cruel but it did lend to her resenting my figure compared to hers or reassuring me she had many male admires when she was my age, and then telling anyone who would listen that I get my looks from her, and then the following awkwardness when she produced the photo albums for proof. But she was amazing. Still, I was a daddy's girl.

I was untouchable when he was alive, almost to the point it was a burden. I had to be very careful about who I moaned about, or how much context I put into a story because if my father thought a man was being mean to me, be it colleague, boyfriend, friend, manager, teacher, whoever, he would start planning their murder. Not in a literal sense, but he would beat someone so badly they would leave the city and never comeback, and the victim knew they had a steel works factory full of old boys who would guarantee it.

While it felt cosy in my youth, it became burdensome as I feared how much he might hurt someone, essentially, I was scared he would one day go too far and end up in prison because of me. I guess any parent wouldn't think twice about killing someone who posed a threat to their offspring, that is probably human instinct, but I loved my dad and valued his place at Sunday dinner more than being bothered by a 'man' with incel vibes.

He once had Nathan by throat, and he did not even know the full story, he just saw enough and what he saw he did not like. I was going to my parent's house for tea after work, Nathan had been sat on the bus too, he did this a lot during this period in time, and on this occasion, he made the mistake of following me off the bus and walking behind me.

When I knew he was behind me I would automatically wrap my arms around myself, I think I was hugging the feeling of worry, and it made it feel warm rather than spikey and it would essentially fade away. A technique people with anxiety practice where they put their hand where they can feel their anxiety to calm it, to own it.

My dad must have seen this from the window and came storming out the house to meet me.

"What's wrong love?"

"Nothing dad, let's just go in…"

"Who the fuck is that?"

"No one dad, please leave it".

"Has he been bothering you?" I didn't even have time to answer, "Now then cunt, who the fuck are you? What have you been doing to my daughter"?

Nathan did not break away from the fantasy world he clearly inhibits "Hello sir, I'm your daughters..." my dad pushed him in the chest.

"I don't give a fuck who you think you are, I know my daughter, and I can see from her body language that you are making her uncomfortable" he pushed him in the chest again, they must have moved about 20 metres backwards already.

Had it not been for my distain I would have been impressed by Nathans resolve and confidence, just the fact he wasn't terrified was extraordinary, he continued trying to reason with my dad, "sir please, if you would just let me explain, sir please stop pushing me…I can see where she gets her aggression and strength from" at this my dad snapped, grabbing him by the throat and throwing him up against the bus stop causing it shake.

"Was that supposed to be funny you weasel?"

Nathan replied with only a slight croak that his crushed windpipe would allow, "yes…sir, it was a joke…I'm…"

"SHUT UP" my dad drew back his fist, ready to make facial plate smear against steel and aluminium, I quickly grabbed his arm "dad stop, just stop now, I said leave it, can we go inside please? DAD" he relented, he could see I was upset and knew hitting Nathan could escalate things, so he looked me in the eyes and eased off, the look he gave me was as if to say, okay I'll stop but only because you asked me to.

As this wrapped up a bus came towards the stop and my dad had his final say "Right you rat, I don't know where this bus goes, and I couldn't give a fuck either, you're going to get on it and fuck off. If I see you on this street or anywhere near my daughter again, you're a dead man, I hope that is clear".

Nathan climbed onto the bus and paid his fare, he then turned to us before the doors closed, I instinctively recoiled causing my dad to wrap his arm around me. Nathan said, "Charmed to have met you sir", the doors closed, the bus left, I saw his silhouette sitting down. My dad just muttered "prick" under his breath, and we walked back the house "finally met your stalker then" he said and winked at me.

When my dad died, I felt an intense vulnerability as well as a tremendous loss. Like a political head I would never want to push the nuclear button, but it was good to have there as a deterrent. I feel a bit gross for having thought like that, I hate war, nuclear threat, and politicians for that matter. Still, I suppose it is an effective metaphor for how I was feeling.

The week leading up to the funeral was a blur, and every other cliché you can think of, I lost my will to survive, walking around without my body armour. I felt ridiculous at times, I would not even see my dad every week, I would sometimes go days upon days without texting him, we had very independent lives. But now those options were no longer available, I was heartbroken.

On the day of the funeral, I stood at the front with my mother, my brothers, and their partners, all united in our sorrow but determined to give him the celebration his life deserved. I took a moment to look across at all the faces, so many friends, so many lives he touched I scanned across the back of the room, and I couldn't believe it, Nathan was stood there, in a black suit and tie, faux mourning a man who would have pummelled him to death had I told him everything. I locked in on him, a tear strolling down my face, half devastated at the violation of him attending my dad's funeral, half raging and intent on giving him a glare so that he knows I am not scared of him, and that I wanted to kill him for this.

I began spiralling and thinking without logic, like there should be laws to stalking beyond the obvious don't do it. If you are going to do it you can ruin my life at the following places, but don't you dare turn up at a funeral. My dad's funeral. I thought breaking into my house had majorly crossed the line, and in fairness it did, but this violation is the absolute worst. How dare he.

Nathen did scurry off like the rodent he is before the end of the funeral, he had the audacity to seem preoccupied by something more important. Which meant him turning up to the funeral to attempt making me feel trapped was secondary to something else in his mind. I don't think I can attribute any mental illness to his actions, and it would be unfair on those who suffer it if I did, he was just a nasty bastard.

I returned to my house after the wake and necked a glass of wine and then threw the glass at the wall watching it shatter and rain diamond splints to the floor beneath. I didn't scream though I did intend to. I grabbed the large kitchen knife from the drawer having thought about nothing else than killing Nathan all the way home from the funeral. A silver lining to having a stalker is that you don't have to go looking for them, they'll come to you.

He did eventually turn up, it was fate, he may have walked past my house often, sometimes several times a night, but he never came up to the door, he never knocked, the idiot wants to be stabbed. I took a deep breath and began unlocking the door, this is for you dad.

I opened the door, and he stood behind a huge box, I simply stood there, tired and confused.

"Hey, I know it's been a tough day for you, well, for all of us actually. But I just wanted to drop this off and then I will come and set it up another day or evening, whenever really".

"What is it? I don't understand?"

"Oh, silly me" he span the box around so I could see the image plastered across the label, "Tada! It's the cot, I promised I would sort it out".

"A cot?" my grip on the knife handle remained as did the intent to cause harm, but the predicament had caught me off guard. "Why have you brought a cot to my house?" I was about to volley some verbal abuse towards him, but he once again surprised me, and not pleasantly.

"You mean, our house, and for our baby of course, are you okay Hun? I know you really miss your dad" he then stood to the side, grinning manically revealing a parked pram with a pumpkin sat inside the base, two eyes and a smile had been scribbled on with a black marker pen.

I dropped the knife and slammed the door shut, locking it as it as it slammed shut. I then slowly slid down the door frame crying, I cried so much that my eyes began to sting as the tear ducts had a reintroduction to sadness following the funeral. I picked the knife up again and gripped it as I hugged my knees, if he tries to break in another way, I will stab him I promised myself, but he just spoke through the door. "I know it has been a really tough day for you Hun, and you have been so strong. I really am proud of you. Look, me, and the baby will go back to my house, but we will come home soon, I think you could benefit from some alone time. Anyway bye, love you…Mummy".

I heard him take the break off the pram and walk away. I cried into my knees and didn't move from that spot for most of the night. I had crossed over from sick and appalled to terrified. And now my dad is gone I have to fight this alone. Every time I closed my eyes, I saw the drawn-on eyes of the pumpkin looking back at me. What kind of sickness had I become tangled up in?

Chapter 26

I worked my way down to the kitchen, I felt good, and even though I knew a storm was brewing, I felt relaxed and ready, ready for whatever. I feel more in tune with the island, I feel like I am a part of Melas. I can sense how far the roots run from the trees under the ground, like I could close my eyes and perfectly navigate their intricate yet complex mapping. I can feel the tide and sense when a wave crashes harsher than the others. All the aspects of my past seemed pointless, like they were things I had to experience to be truly born where I am supposed to be, the whole stalking thing seemed almost trivial. I am now part of something bigger. More important.

I did not want a coffee this morning, I opted for some water, I strolled to the bottom of the garden to behind the bushes where the stream is. I had not even considered the garden of the cottage before, beyond an acknowledgement of it being a beautiful surrounding. I was not aware of the stream here until I felt it. I dipped a cup into the stream and then strolled back to the cottage, sipping the water, and gently waving at the nesting birds in the trees, I am alert to the fact they are watching me, I can feel their presence. Not just in the garden, but throughout miles of forest as well.

I take my cup of water and sit at the kitchen table; it is not perfect clear water, but it is the Melas keeping me hydrated and I am more than grateful for that. The thought of breakfast makes me feel a bit sick, I find cereal too sweet, I think croissants are too dry, and fruit is too juicy, and so I follow my instincts rather than over thinking, I take a bowl of ground Beef mince out of the fridge. With my first handful I can tell it is meat from this island and I devour it raw. It was perfect.

Instead of washing my hands afterwards I committed to my new meaning in life, to be at one with the island. I continuously rubbed my hands together and up and down my forearms letting the fat from the mince offer my skin a protective oily layer.

I closed my eyes so that I could feel the oils from the meat fat slowly commute up my arms and across my body. I could feel the rest of it in my stomach being broken down and the nutrients beginning to strengthen me. At that moment I sensed a disturbance in the woods. A rope was being harnessed around a thick tree branch, a bloodied body being positioned to fall and hang. I know not what had happened prior to this, but knowing the woods were alive with activity made me smile.

How I long to see what could be happening in the woods, be part of whatever it may be. But I know I need to be patient. Right now, I have a purpose and I need to finish this chapter before I can begin anew. I returned to the bedroom, the bed calling out for me to have a snooze, looking more inviting and comfortable than ever before. But I have slept too much, there is work to be done. I opened the wardrobe and greeted my options of clothing with a sneer. This all used to be to my taste. Now it doesn't look right. Jeans are too tight, too restricting. Leggings may offer comfort but are made of harmful materials. There is nothing here I want to wear.

I decide on wearing my dress that I arrived here in. I hate it. But I figure one last outing for it would be quite fitting. No pun intended; it wasn't a tight-fitting dress. That was one aspect that suited my needs today. I did not want anything too constricting that may block the feeling and connection I have to the island. I slide downstairs on the banister for the first time in my life, it came surprisingly natural to me, that or it is just an easy thing to do. I could sense further activity in the forest what exactly wasn't clear, but I could hear harsh sea waves which I assume means the fisherman is close by. The waves sounded aggressive as before, but I was no longer scared, I felt in control, if I concentrated, I could dictate their rhythm.

I walked towards my front door, I felt like I would see if there was anything within a few yards of the cottage happening. As I reached for the door there was an almighty thud from the door to my right, the little door that was locked and full of mystery…I wonder…I skipped towards it, excitement replacing trepidation. Again, it thudded, the closer I got the harsher the shaking of the door became, like it was climaxing. I grabbed the handle and whispered, "it's me" and I heard a lock click, and the door glided open. I was expecting an ominous creak, but it revealed itself without making a sound. In fact, all the noises had stopped. All my senses focused on this entrance. This must be important. The wooden staircase doesn't creak, it's almost like a rough sponge under my feet, I approach the ground, it is a cellar to the cottage, I knew it. The floor was made up of dusty earth, well composted mud, I knelt and let it run through my fingers before tasting it. Rich earth, the nutrition and minerals contained within spreading through my body. My next step lit up the room as lanterns burst into flames to reveal a symbol scribed in the mud, ah yes, the symbol. I just smiled and chuckled to myself.

I looked across the room and saw there was a small wooden table and on it was an item, I could not quite distinguish what as the flicker of the flame only gave me hints to what it could be. I went over to see, and there was a small knife, its blade almost ending in a pinprick. Next to the knife was golden plate, as I looked at the blade a whisper was ringing in my ears "*do it, do it*" the gold plate also contained the symbol that was harshly dragged through the mud beneath me, the plate wanted some of my blood, and I owed it that much, it was the least I could do.

I grabbed the knife and slowly pulled up the sleeve of my dress, the whisper grew louder and more drawn out "*doooooo ittttt, DO ITTTTTTT!!!*" I kissed the blade and was about to run it through my skin before a different stabbing pain interrupted this ritual, the pain jolted across the back of my skull and through my temple, I dropped the knife and looked towards the door, I had to get back upstairs quickly, I can sense it. Nathan is here.

Chapter 27

I could smell the oil in the lanterns begin to burn in the room next to the one I was occupying, he is here, he is in my cottage. He has broken into a property of mine again. I continuously heard a whisper from around the room "*kill*", in the trees surrounding the cottage I could hear crows begin to squawk, they sounded excited, I was excited, it is time to finally finish that part of my life. Freedom, real freedom, is not far away.

The door opened, he strolled in, lost, confused, and covered in dirt and blood, the woods had given him a good slapping on the way here, good on them. He then laid eyes on me, he looked happy, he looked relieved. He is supposed to be scared. He spoke; "Lainya? Oh my god Lainya, it's really you" each time he said that name it caused a stabbing pain in my head, why the fuck is he calling me that?!

The whispers around the room counterbalanced his nonsense saying "*Sylvia, be strong, Sylvia do what must be done*", Nathan continued "It's really you. I knew it, I knew you weren't dead. Are you okay are you hurt? I've been looking for…" having him talk while the whispers tried to guide me, while the Crows sang their song in the trees outside was all too much and I just instinctively responded, "I'm fine".

Nathan looked awkward and concerned for me, "Is there anyone else here? Are you safe? How did you…" the whispers countered every word out of his mouth "*kill him, finish this!*" Again, there is too many stimuli at once and I snap "I said, I'm fine". He now seemed to be getting agitated, presumably pissed off he hasn't managed to stalk me for a while. Pathetic. He seems to be objecting to my lack of response to him and takes a step towards my direction, it was a small step, but it made my body react and it hurt, like a paper cut but a big one straight down my middle. "Stay the fuck back, don't fucking come near me".

Again, he seems perplexed that I do not want him near me, like he hadn't received the memo by now. He spoke "Lainya?! Sweetheart?". Again, hearing that name causes a stabbing pain in my head, why is he doing this, why is he trying to hurt me? "Stop calling me sweetheart, and stop fucking calling Lainya, that is not my name". My body shakes as adrenaline rushes through me, and he tries to control the situation "Okay, okay, let's just talk. What is your name?"

"Sylvia, I know it is old fashioned but that has always been my name. It didn't suit me as a baby, but I am growing into it".

"Right, Sylvia, do you know who I am?"

"Yes, of course!"

He smiles at this, like he has won something, like me knowing who he is, is an achievement, so I continue as the whispers encourage me to do so, "You are a living nightmare, a curse I cannot wash off. I came here to escape you. But here you fucking are, as always! Stalking me, day, and night, all through Sheffield, and now over fucking seas!"

"Lain…sorry, Sylvia. I am your husband. We are married. We are here on holiday. If you could let me, come a little closer, I can show you photos from our wedding day".

He shuffles forward, just a centre metre and again a pain slices through me "I told you to stay back, do not come near me. How did you even find me? I thought this would be the end of this bullshit. Why can't you just go away?"

"I am not leaving you here, and I hope one day you will thank me for that". Now why on earth would I do that, the whispers rationalise his madness "*he's trying to trick you, it's all lies, he wants to hurt you, you cannot trust him*". I could tell he was now getting desperate and really trying to force his manipulation of me, "What about our daughter? We have a little girl, surely you remember her?"

"You really are a sick fuck. Don't you ever attribute that thing to me ever again! That pumpkin you carry around, pretending it's a child, our child?! Listen, loon, I am not your wife, and we have not had a baby together. That pumpkin you carry around should be nothing more than Halloween decoration. Listen, I am sorry, you are clearly, clearly, mentally unwell. I do not know if you have had a breakdown, or if you have always been a nut case, but all this, all this stalking me needs to stop. It has been years! You've made my life hell. I have begged you to leave me alone, my father told you to leave me alone Everywhere I turn, you are there. I thought I had finally gotten away from you."

At this he becomes more passionate in his argument, he is mad that I am not falling for it, that I can see through his lies, he knows he can't grab me and shove engagement rings on my finger and storm off, he knows this time it is different, that the island has chosen me and that it will protect me.

He counters my rant ""Don't you dare talk about our baby like that! This is absurd, I am not your stalker, we dated, we got engaged, we got married, had a baby, and more recently we went on a holiday. And I do not know what the fuck has happened Lainya but please just fucking trust me, let's get out of here, please let me help you. We can go somewhere, and we can just talk and figure everything out" the whispers warn me "*do not go with him, he will hurt you, you're safe here, he wants to hurt you*".

I wince as he calls me 'Lainya' again, and he takes some more steps towards me, each step slices through me like a fresh wound, I need to stop him, the whispers guide me "the drawer, look in the drawer, gun there, protect yourself".

Nathan is gob smacked when I produce the gun and point it right at his fucking face, the gun that was left for me at the lighthouse, precisely for this moment. "Stop right there! This is your final warning, you are not my husband, you are a very Ill man, and you have been stalking me and tormenting me for years. The police know that I am here, that is why this place is so remote, you shouldn't have been able to find me. You have two choices now, turn away and leave me the fuck alone, forever. Or you carry on this bullshit, and I fucking kill you. I don't want to do that, but I will, one way or another it ends tonight, please don't make me shoot you, just walk away".

"*No, you mustn't let him leave! You will never truly be free he has to die; you must kill him*".

"I am not a stalker, I am your husband, please just calm down and let me help you".

"*Lies, he lies, he wants to hurt you, shoot him!*"

"Anytime I go anywhere you are there lagging behind, you turn up outside my work, you broke into my house, you turned up at my fucking dad's funeral. You have been a living nightmare, please Nathan, please just walk away".

"This, this is insane. Please, just let me help you, I can't just leave you here, please I am begging you just let me help you, we will get through this together, I can't just leave you here. I know you don't want to hurt me, and you know I would never do anything to hurt you"

He steps towards me, hands aloft, almost like he wants to be a target, he steps forward and contemplates another step, the pain it causes me almost makes me drop the gun, the whispers support me through this trauma "*Shoot him, do it, shoot him now!*". We make eye contact for a fleeting second, his eyes widen as I pull on the trigger, before his facial features are sucked into a tiny black hole caused by his skull exploding its contents onto my floor as a bullet penetrates his face. His body falls back at the force of the blast, and it is over. I have killed him.

Chapter 28

I speak aloud "well, that is messier than I had contemplated" I waited for the whisper to respond, but it didn't, once again there was perfect silence, the crows had frozen, the breeze and ocean had muted, I spoke again "now what?". Still nothing, I guess I need to figure out the next steps on my own. I walked over Nathans carcass and dip my finger in some of the blood to try it, it tasted toxic, I will drag it out to the woods this evening and let nature decide what to do with it.

As I step forward, I can sense I am being drawn back to the cellar, there is perfect silence until I turn in the direction of the cellar door and then a vacuum sound appears, it is like I am being wrapped in plastic and pulled towards the opening. The Knife, the plate, the symbol, of course, I have unfinished business down there, I was interrupted my Nathan. I must finish down there.

I continue in a daze towards the door, but then notice how perfectly frozen the outside of the cottage looks. The birds aren't moving, the trees are perfectly still, no hint of wind or slight breeze, what the hell, there is a butterfly in suspended animation. What is happening? I decided I must investigate this before I do anything further.

It feels like the house is objecting. Nothing visible is happening but it feels like both my ankles are shackled, and each step is heavy. But the more I am restricted the more I feel intrigued by what is happening outside. At this the whispers reappear *"Stay, don't go outside, it is safer here, come down here, join us"* I respond, "I won't be long, I'll be right back my darlings". I walk out the front door.

The vibe has shifted, something feels wrong, I approach the little fence that seals in my front garden and get knocked back and land on my back with a thud. I don't understand, I am supposed to be free now, I am no longer a prisoner, I no longer have a stalker. I get up and walk towards the fence, this time I command it "I refuse your protection, let me free" it opens, and I step into the woods.

I look around, nothing seems out of the ordinary, then I hear a voice, my voice, She-Me!

"So, you reject us?"

"What? No…I just…"

"After everything we have done to protect you, to help you, you reject us".

"I haven't…I just wanted…"

"You just wanted to do what you want and fuck everyone else, we know"

"She-Me, where are you?"

"I'm up here Sylvia, or should I say Lainya".

I crease over in pain, my head feeling like my brain is swelling beyond my skull's capacity, I look up and she is stood in the tree, holding the book which had been sent to my house months ago.

"I just wanted to explore the forest, enjoy my freedom, please I'll go back to the cellar now" I spin around and get to my feet, but the cottage is gone, there is just a mound of earth, and a cave within, oh my god, it is the exact cave I was having nightmares about at home. Maybe they weren't nightmares, could they have been warnings?

I shout up the tree, "What's happening? Please help me, I'll do anything you ask"

"It is too late for that Lainya, you aren't worthy" she holds aloft the book and rips out the page that contained my blood, at this is scream in agony. She then rips the page down the middle perfectly splitting it and says, "goodbye gorgeous" and winks at me.

Quicker than I can react two trees use their branches and wrap around my arms and legs, I couldn't escape the grip, the wood was thick but could move like a vine whip, they begin to pull me in separate directions, all I can think about is Nathan and our dau…

EPILOGUE

1

"Jesus, what a mess, a bloody mess, literally"

"Oh, have some fucking respect will ya".

"Sir?"

"Respect! For the dead, it shouldn't be a hard concept for you to understand".

"That's fair, apologies sir".

"Don't mention it".

"Still, how often do you see a body that has been pulled or ripped perfectly in half, what the hell would have caused this?"

"No idea Rook". I knew exactly what caused this, I've seen it before, but I can't tell him, I shouldn't have brought him with me. As soon as I knew it was an incident in the woods I should have come alone.

"Speaking of respect sir…"

"Yeah?"

"I've been in the police for 8 years and worked with you for 18 months, do you have to call me Rook?"

"What's wrong with that name?"

"Well, I would say I am long serving, not a rookie".

"I call you Rook because your surname is Rooker".

"Oh, my mistake, sorry sir".

"No problem, Rookie".

"Sir?"

"I'm just kidding, let some go will ya, for fucks sake". I'm using humour to deflect from the evil that is happening here, there is a nervousness in my voice which might be a giveaway. He is a good cop; I think he has a promising career. I do not want this to destroy that.

"C'mon Rook, let forensics get the photo's we'll head back to mainland".

"If it's okay sir I'd like to stay a little bit longer".

"Why?"

"Well, I have never worked on anything like this before, I know it is, erm…gruesome, but it is kind of a unique crime scene. I just think it would be a good learning experience y'know?"

"It is definitely gruesome, and that's coming from me, I worked on the Edward Miles case".

"You worked on Edward Miles?"

"Yeah" he seems distracted now, maybe if I start walking, he will instinctively follow.

"I watched a documentary on that case the other night, how come you didn't feature on it?"

"I'll tell you why Rook, because of all those people that died, that's why, forgive me for shying away from the celebrity status but I didn't find it very fucking entertaining. It was a horrible time to be doing this job, I'll tell ya".

"Sorry"

"Don't mention it, c'mon let's get out of here". I take a few steps, I notice the symbol etched into a tree, I don't acknowledge it a second longer or give it a further glance. I don't want Rook to see it. He is a good detective, he may notice it anyway, but he damn sure isn't going to see it because I've pointed it out to him. I realise that he isn't following me, "Rook?"

"Sir, you go ahead I really want to investigate further".

"Permission denied, I need you back at the station".

"With the greatest respect I do not need your permission and I am going to stay a little longer".

I smile, I can't help it, he is meeting his potential, he is listening to his gut and not me, I would have done the same at his age, just a shame he can't see I am trying to protect him. "See you back at the station then". I give him a lingering look, hoping he would read between the lines. He looks back at me, he is not getting it, I think he's creeped out that I am now to staring into his eyes. I have to leave him.

I take about 14 steps before Rook calls out for me, "Sir, back here quickly". My stomach drops, I normally hear that said several times a day but hearing it in this forest means it'll be for a reason that ranges from haunting to unexplainable. I am hoping for the latter, it's easier to paper over those cracks and move on from, it won't cause a promising career to end abruptly. I think all this while sprinting right back to where I was stood just 10 seconds ago, dodging tree roots that seem to want to trip me.

"What is it? What have you seen?"

"There in the cave".

I walk into the cave, being greeted as I do so by a repugnant smell that almost makes me reluctant to explore further, but I see a man on the floor, he has been shot in the face. I instinctively begin pulling on my detested Nitrile gloves. They are perfect for the job, but they really dry my skin out, and I already have stiffening hands from arthritis. I stand over the body, beginning to talk to him in my mind 'forgive me mate, I am going to need to have a rummage in your pocket for some ID'. Rook joins me, twanging the stretchy end of his glove so it snaps at his wrist.

"It's a body sir".

"Yes…thank you Rook, thank God you were here".

"Sorry sir".

2

I crouch down, feeling like a bastard for enjoying my own sarcasm so much. The guy has a phone in his pocket, I push the home button and recognise the screen instantly having held this very phone before. I stand up and turn to Rook with a huge sigh, half to prep myself for the debrief I am about to give, half to disguise the pain in my lower back and knees for affording the luxury of bending down for 8 seconds.

"Remember when we went to the B&B to talk to that Nathan bloke?"

"The guy with the missing wife? Is that him?"

"I am afraid so".

"So, the body out front is…"

"Yep, I guess he found his wife, obviously we need to confirm this, but my intuition tells me that is the case, and I have been doing this long enough to trust my gut".

"Well then what the fuck has happened? Two holiday makers come to Melas, the wife goes missing, so the husband searches, then she ends up split in fucking two and he ends up with his face blown off".

"Seems an accurate summary yes".

"Sir what the fuck?"

"Rook, calm down, I need you to be think clearly, I am sorry but your emotions are your enemy right now".

"Fuck, I am sorry sir, you're right".

"Are you okay?" He isn't of course he isn't this is pure insanity, "hey, look at me, Rook just stay with me long enough to get back to the station, you can blow off some steam then, okay?"

"Yeah".

I turn to walk back to where the lady was split in two, I need to ask forensics to run some more specific tests on the remains. Rook shouts after me, "Didn't they have a baby?"

"Yep, they did". I respond but I don't stop walking, I need him to follow me out of this cave, get back outside and get some air. I walk towards the mouth of the cave with my head down to concentrate on what is behind me and ensure Rook is following. Upon reaching this destination I hear the sound of a gun being cocked.

3

I spin around to face Rook, his eyes look completely glazed over, like he is in shock, or fighting some internal demon, his arms hang limply by his side, his fingers just about wrap around his gun handle which he has just readied to shoot.

"Rook? Rook, what are you doing?" He doesn't reply, he isn't even looking at me, his eyes are fixed over my shoulder, "Rook why have you readied you gun? Rook??". He slowly lifts the gun, steadies himself and points it at me, ready to shoot. I have completely mistaken his demeanour, he is scared. "Rook, put the gun down, come over here and talk to me, we can both walk out of here and get back to work, nothing crazy needs to happen".

He pulls back the trigger, readying to shoot a bullet. "Rook, do not fire that gun, I command you to stop!" He points the gun away from me only by about 15 centimetres, but he seems to be more like himself, his body language tells me that he is in full control, it as if his soul temporarily left his body and has now returned. Finally, he speaks.

"Don't move! Put your hands up!"

"Rook?"

He steps to the side, and continues, "I said, put your fucking hands up" I turn around, he isn't talking to me. Behind me stands four women, one is wearing a cloak which dresses her bad disfigurement, such wounds that should mean she is dead, and by her side three unkept women, old, overweight, dirty clothing and menacing glares directed straight at Rook, shit. I know these women, I have met them twice before, and instantly this is a red alert. Rook has no idea.

"Rook lower your weapon now" he does nothing and remains holding aloft his gun.

"ROOK PUT YOUR FUCKING GUN DOWN NOW!"

"Sir, no! I can't"

"PUT IT DOWN, THAT'S AN ORDER FROM A SUPERIOR".

"Sir something's wrong, I need you to trust me".

"Rook, you have no idea what you're doing, please lower your weapon".

"But sir…"

Fuck this, I pull out my own gun and within a second, I have fired his gun out of his hand, I don't hit his hand or fingers, but his hand and wrist will be badly bruised for a couple of weeks. He won't be able to fire his weapon during this time, but I did what had to be done.

"Sir what the hell, WHY DID YOU DO THAT, YOU HAVE NO RIGHT?" he calls me a prick under his breath, he reaches around his back for his handcuffs wincing at the pain in his hand which is already swollen to almost double its size. He storms towards the women, I assume he wants to arrest them, I admire his commitment, I am equally frustrated by his stubbornness.

"Rook, stop right there, do not go any further" he doesn't break his stride, "Rook listen to me". He is pissed off, he isn't listening. Shit, this is going to be horrible. I jog backwards so that I am stood between Rook and the four women. I point my gun at his face, "Rook fucking stop now, I mean it Rook, fall back now!" He slows slightly, "why are you protecting these bitches?".

"Shut up Rook, not another word, do you hear me, not another word" he continues walking, I sense he is unsure what to do, unsure of if I would actually shoot him or not.

"What's happening, why are you protecting these…these…these…"

Sometimes you need to escalate matters before you can calm them, I gun buck Rook on the side of his head, he is going to have a swollen cheekbone to counterbalance his hand, he falls to the floor unconscious and lays there slumped in a heap. Now, straight into damage control mode, I throw my gun to the side and drop to my knees but poise my body up, holding both hands aloft. I am terrified but I do not want to show it, foolish pride I guess, male pride, toxic bullshit.

"I've tossed my weapon; I am no threat" they just stare back at me.

"I am so sorry, I thought we had an agreement, you aren't usually this…this messy".

The lady in the cloak steps forward, for a split second her face takes Rook's form before returning to her disfigured, rotting appearance. "Such a nasty boy he is darling, such a mean, mean man".

"No! Please, sorry, he isn't bad, he's a good person, he means well, please, he is…look he's a fucking good cop just please leave him alone. If you want to punish someone punish me".

She looks at me just long enough to pretend she's contemplating the request before smirking and saying "no". The other three let out a giggle. One claps together her hands and says "mean boy, mean, mean boy" another says "splash the captains boat snaps, splash a fish boat sinks" that's all she ever says. I need to fix this.

"Look, let's stick to our agreement yeah? You've made a mess, but I can make all this go away, we won't bother you. You stick to your side of the agreement, and we'll stick to ours".

The only one to have not spoken gives me a simple command, "leave our cave now" I nod, I grab Rook dragging him along the floor and out of the cave with me. This is young man's game; I don't know how much longer my body can endure this. As we pass them, I speak when perhaps I shouldn't "why did you cause that to happen to them?". They all stare at me in silence. I carry on dragging Rook out of the cave before one of them appears in front me, as if out of nowhere, "we were bored! Okay? Now fuck off!!".

They erupt into a harrowing laughter that makes me feel sick, it is a noise that I already know will haunt me, I just know it. As I exit the cave, I can hear them laughing and saying "horrible boy! What a wicked man!!" ""splash the captains boat snaps, splash a fish boat sinks". I will never forgive myself for involving Rook in this.

4

I eventually get Rook to what I would consider a safe enough distance from the cave and use some smelling salts to wake him. I then sit on the ground beside him as he slowly comes round and familiarises himself with his environment. I crouch close to him to appear supportive and comforting but the truth is I need a breather and dragging his arse across the woods was not on the agenda today. I am also worried, no, scared, at what we may have just started in that cave.

"Why did you sucker punch me?"

I smile and roll my shoulders slightly as I have a little laugh which never materialises into an audible sound. "If you want to tell people that was a sucker punch then I am okay with that. I notice him looking at his hands and attempting to flex his fingers gently. "Sorry about the hand, you need to follow my lead a bit better".

"Sir" I knew what he was going to ask me before I he even spoke, and I interject "I was not protecting those women; I was protecting you. I'm happy to try and explain what happened Rook but not here, it's not safe. Back at the car you can ask any questions".

"Let me guess, the trees have ears, right?" he smirks.

"And mouths and arms, now c'mon, let's get out of here. This place gives me the creeps". He laughs a little, but I also notice him have a quick glance around.

As we continue our trek out of the woodland and back to the car, Rook is sweating profusely, and complaining his head hurts. Maybe I hit him too hard. "There's water in the car Rook, just hold on, not far to go now".

Finally, we get back to the car I slump into the drivers' seat and, push the chair back and close my eyes, I have no desire to drive back right away, I feel like I could sleep for 10 hours. I loosen my tie and unbutton the top button of my collar to allow my windpipe the luxury of inhaling with no restriction. Rook slowly slides down to his seat on the passenger side "I don't feel so good sir, I might hijack a cell back at the station and have a snooze".

"Not until you have been to the hospital, you need to be checked out".

"I'll be fine, just tired battered and bruised".

"We'll let the doctor decide if you're okay, c'mon, let's get going, it's been a harsh day, and the sooner you get checked out the quicker we can get home".

He fell silent, leaning in his seat, I think he might be asleep already. I open his window slightly as he is still sweating to an extent that suggests he has a harsh fever. As I begin driving, he murmurs slightly, and then begins talking, while keeping his eyes closed, like a toddler trying to fight falling to sleep.

"Sir, why did you think I needed protection from those women? Why did you shoot the gun out of my hand? Are you corrupt?"

"No Rook, I am not corrupt, far from it actually. Sometimes things happen on this island that simply can't be explained, and it would be a waste of police time and resources to try and investigate it. Furthermore, an investigation would be opening a can worms and kick start a war that we would have no hope of winning. To protect this island, its people, and its history it is better we put our resource into prevention rather than investigation".

"I do not understand, we met with that guy, Nathan I think he was called, before he had his head blown off, why didn't we save him then?"

"I didn't know it would end like this, I was scared it might, but trying to protect him that early on and give him the rationale as to why, again, it's a can of worms Rook, we have a duty to protect the people of Melas, sometimes that protection can be withholding information that could be harmful. What do we say, oh sir it is best you stop looking for your missing wife. She's gone, c'mon I'll buy you a beer. That is not going to work is it".

"We should go back, arrest them, put a stop to whatever this is".

"You don't think I'd have already fucking done that if it were that simple, you think I enjoy having all these bodies I have to just sweep under a rug? It goes against my better judgement, my morals, and my practice Rook, but we have an agreement".

"You made an agreement with them?"

"Listen, this is way bigger than me, I'm just the unlucky bastard that has to carry this on, but in a nutshell, we leave them alone, they leave us alone. That's the way it must be. I don't like it but trust me we would not win a fight with them. It would just be pest control for them".

"Sir" he is now wincing in pain, as if each bead of sweat is causing him agony, as if each word takes tremendous effort to articulate, "there's stuff you're not telling me"

"You're damn right there is, and with good reason. Listen I trust you, I value your opinion, but like I said, this is bigger than me. It's bigger than the police. I am sworn to secrecy, and you've already seen and know way too much. We're going to keep that much between us Rook, I don't need your body on my conscience".

"Why do you keep calling me Rook?"

"I told ya earlier today, because your surname is…"

"MY FUCKING NAME IS DRUDNER"

5

No, no, no, no! Shit. Now we're in trouble. I glance at him, he is just staring at me, he then leans forward in his seat and throws up in the footwell, mostly sea water, some maggots. "Stay with me Rook"

"My name is Drudner! Say. My. Name! SAY IT."

"No."

"Say it."

"No."

My resistance in saying what he thinks is his proper name is making him angry. I have been through this before, but I am still at a loss what to do, I don't know if going to the hospital is still wise or if it would endanger more people, so I'll continue driving to somewhere remote, see if I can have a proper conversation.

"Sir."

"Yes Rook."

He snarls as I use his name, "why did you shoot me?"

"I had to get the gun out of your hand".

"No not that, the leg. Why did you shoot me in the fucking leg?"

"Wha-what are you…what are you talking about? I've never shot you in the leg. I've never put a bullet in you".

"YES, YOU HAVE, you're a liar, you fucking shot me, tried to disable me".

"LISTEN, I HAVE NEVER SHOT YOU. Shit, take off your trousers and look, you've never been shot in the leg".

"YES, I HAVE, YOU DID IT" he then grabs a gun that was laying in a holster on the backseat of the car and screams "YOU SHOT ME RIGHT HERE" and fires the gun into his own leg, too fast for me to react. "SHIT!!!" I swerve on and off the road about 5 times and then pull up on an empty grass verge by the road, the sound of the gun blast still ringing in my ears. Goddammit, this has escalated way too fast. He's grabbing his leg tight, applying pressure to his own wound. Brave man, or perhaps a lunatic. He grimaces and is laughing, could be shock.

"You shot me in the leg you bastard, you wanted to kill me".

"No, I didn't, why would I want you dead? You're my partner".

"Because of my wife."

"What?!"

"You think I'm stupid, I've seen the way you look at her".

"Rook, I have never seen your wife. I have a wife of my own, listen, I'm not a cheat, I'm not trying to kill you, and I am going to help you, but you have to listen to me".

"Drudner."

"Rook stop it. Listen to me, your memories, the things you think happened, didn't! Your head is going to be full of false memories, you have to believe me".

"Why don't you listen to me, fucking pig! My name is Drudner, you never wanted me on the force, you tried to kill me, shot me in leg, right fucking here LOOK! But that wasn't enough, you followed me home, tried to have sex with my wife. THEN, then when my parents went missing you killed the case, made it impossible for me to find them".

"Rook, this is all wrong, we found your parents, it was that day I made you my partner, I could see what a good soul you were".

"LIAR!"

"I'm not lying, I need you to trust me. Your memories have been warped, this stuff did happen, just not as you remember it. Damn, Rook, we're partners, we're friends, you have got to remember this somewhere? I am not your enemy, just remember!"

"MY NAME IS DRUDNER"

"Okay Drudner, well tell me this, what is your son's name?"

His face drops, this landed, his eyes shoot from side to side, his mind is racing, "M…my…my…s…son…"

"What's his name, come on, I know you remember".

"I…I…" he folds over in pain, gripping his head so tight I can see he is beginning to pull his own hair out, he then let's out a scream. He swiftly shoots back up and grabs me by the jaw, crushing my head against the driver window causing it to crack and cutting the back of my head. Now I'm pissed off. I grab his wrist and manage to uppercut him hard enough to make him fall back slightly, I then let go of his wrist and hit him clean across the jaw. His head spins and hits the window and he remains motionless resting his forehead against the window.

"You can tell people that was a sucker punch as well if you like".

He laughs but remains resting his head against his window. He looks up slowly and I can see he is just watching the waves roll back and forth. For all the drama that has unfolded I did manage to stumble across a picturesque setting. There is a little fishing boat making its way back to land, maybe about 2 miles off. Must be done for the day. I want to ask Rook if he remembers his son's name, but truth be told I am enjoying these few seconds of calm.

END?

It is short lived, it always is. Rook notices the boat and he turns to me, a smile spreads across his face, a sickening smile, it seems to continue spreading, getting wider than I thought would be possible, like I had a case of prosopometamorphopsia. It is something else that will haunt me from this dreadful day. He is thinking of something, but I know I am not going to like it. He glances back at the boat, and then back to me and just says in a voice which only has an inkling of his actual voice counterbalanced by a deep growl "snap goes the boat, splash!"

"Rook! Don't…". The gun he used to shoot himself in the leg is span around in his hand and the handle hurtles towards my face.

I wake up, groggy, head thumping, and severely dehydrated. I hear commotion and I look across to the beach and see a crowd has gathered, there is a few of my guys down there as well. What the hell did you do Rook? And where the hell are ya? What happened to that boat? I look forward and the windscreen is fogged up with condensation, the words 'what a wicked man' have been drawn across the glass.

I punch the steering wheel in anger and frustration.

"Fucking witches"

Printed in Great Britain
by Amazon